# Haunted Hamlet

by

## Kathi Daley

This book is a work of fiction. Names, characters, places, and incidents either are products of the author's imagination or are used fictitiously. Any resemblance to actual events or locales or persons, living or dead, is entirely coincidental.

Copyright © 2014 by Katherine Daley

Version 1.0

This book is dedicated to Jessica Fischer, who jumped in to help me out when I commented on my Facebook page that I was having difficulty with the cover image for this book. You know what they say about it taking a village. Thank you, Jessica, for being part of my village.

I also want to thank Amy Brantley for her contribution of the recipe for loaded mashed potato bread.

And I must mention my team of advance readers for taking time out of their busy lives to help me launch each new book and the awesome bloggers in my life for helping me publicize them.

And, as always, love and thanks to my sister Christy for her time, encouragement, and unwavering support. I also want to thank Carrie, Cristin, Brennen, and Danny for the Facebook shares, Randy Ladenheim-Gil for the editing, and, last but not least, my super-husband Ken for allowing me time to write by taking care of everything else.

# Books by Kathi Daley

**Paradise Lake Series:**
*Pumpkins in Paradise*
*Snowmen in Paradise*
*Bikinis in Paradise*
*Christmas in Paradise* – Sept. 2014

**Zoe Donovan Mysteries:**
*Halloween Hijinks*
*The Trouble With Turkeys*
*Christmas Crazy*
*Cupid's Curse*
*Big Bunny Bump-off*
*Beach Blanket Barbie*
*Maui Madness*
*Derby Divas*
*Haunted Hamlet*
*Turkeys, Tuxes, and Tabbies*– October 2014
*Christmas Cozy* – November 2014

**Road to Christmas Romance:**
*Road to Christmas Past*

# Chapter 1

## Friday, October 17

Halloween is my favorite holiday. I know most people don't really get my obsession with all things spooky, but I love everything about this awesome time of year. I love the decorations, the annual events, horror movies on TV, personalized pumpkins, and finding the scariest costume of all. But it's not just the awesomeness of the holiday that I love, it's the coziness of the season. The romance of that first wood fire, hot cider with good friends, hiking through groves of aspens dressed in fall colors, and the scent of snow just around the corner.

"I'm thinking witch." My best friend, Ellie Davis, held up a mask with a huge wart on the nose. She'd been sort of down all week, so I was happy to see her enthusiasm for the pre-holiday shopping trip.

I frowned. "Weren't you a witch last year?"

"And the ten years before that," the third member of our triad, Levi Denton, added.

Ellie shrugged. "It's what I do. Every year: witch."

"Doesn't that seem a little boring?" I wondered.

"I think the word you're searching for is consistent." Ellie smiled.

"Come on, El, you need to make a little effort for the tenth annual Zoe Donovan Halloween Spooktacular," Levi persuaded.

"Technically we missed last year, so this is only the ninth annual Spooktacular," Ellie pointed out.

Ellie was right. Normally, I have a party every year, but last year my plans were interrupted by the discovery of a dead football coach in the basement of a *real* haunted house. The same haunted house, I hate to say, that the Ashton Falls Events Committee voted to use as a venue for this year's Haunted Hamlet.

"Okay, then don't you want to make more of an effort for the ninth annual Spooktacular?" Levi corrected himself.

"Fine." Ellie sighed.

"How about this?" Levi held up a cat costume that was little more than a black unitard with ears and a tail.

"In your dreams." Ellie laughed. "I'm pretty sure that outfit will leave nothing to the imagination, and personally, I like to maintain just a bit of mystery."

"Come on; it's an awesome costume," Levi insisted.

"Then you wear it." Ellie grinned as she poked her index finger into his chest.

"It would show off my boyish figure," Levi teased as he jokingly held it up in front of his sculpted frame. "I have to admit I'm looking quite svelte since I've been putting in extra time at the gym so that I can keep up with Darla."

"Oh please." Ellie rolled her eyes. I knew that Levi's new girlfriend was a sore subject with the woman who had suffered the agony of falling in love with a man she would never have.

"Have you seen where they keep the pus?" I asked in an attempt to change the subject and break the tension.

"Pus? Really?" Ellie put her hands on her hips in disgust. "This is the first big party you and Zak have thrown as a couple. Don't you think you should go for something other than oozing wounds and external entrails?"

"It's Halloween," I pointed out. "Zak will expect pus."

"Personally, I'm thinking I'll woo the crowd with my gentleman pirate imitation," Levi offered as he plopped a pirate hat on his head. After taking a look at Levi, I realized that with his dark, wavy hair grown out, hc had the looks to pull it off. "Would you perchance care to be my lady?" he asked Ellie.

"What about your actual lady?" Ellie responded.

"A pirate can never have too many ladies." Levi wiggled his eyebrows.

"Oh please," Ellie repeated, picking up a plastic parrot and plopping it on Levi's shoulder.

"I was going to be a zombie," I offered, "but they seem so passé."

"If you get the zombie outfit, you can get twice the bang for your buck and use if for the zombie run," Levi pointed out.

"True. I was so busy with the murder investigation last year that I didn't even dress up for the zombie run. This year I plan to be corpse free so I can enjoy all the walking-dead fun."

"Did the guys I sent over from the football team get squared away?" Levi asked.

"Yeah, they're going to be great. Thanks for rounding them up."

Every year as part of the Haunted Hamlet, the town of Ashton Fall's sponsors a zombie run in which participants attempt to complete a five-mile course with volunteers dressed as zombies chasing them. The zombies, who are often members of the high-school football team Levi coaches, try to "kill" the runners by capturing their flags before they cross the finish line. Usually only a handful of runners complete the course alive, but fun is had by all.

"I had a lot more volunteers this year because we don't have a game the night before," Levi commented.

"Why don't we have a game next weekend?" I asked.

Last Halloween Ashton Falls played our biggest rival, and the pregame hijinks the highly anticipated event created caused quite a lot of trouble for everyone involved. It started with friendly pregame pranks and ended with a murder that threatened people and things I hold near and dear.

"We have a bye next weekend," Levi explained. "We play Juniper Valley tomorrow. You're coming?"

"I wouldn't miss it. How's Juniper's record this year?"

"Not as good as ours." Levi grinned.

"Undefeated after five games is quite a feat," I agreed. "I remember last year, when . . ."

"Watch out." Levi grabbed my arm as a group of elementary school–aged boys ran down the aisle, knocking me into the shelving behind me in the process.

"There sure are a lot of kids in here," I commented as I righted myself.

"It is Halloween," Ellie said. "Halloween is a *children's* holiday."

"I guess we should have come in earlier in the day, while the little buggers were in school." Aston Falls is a small town without a lot of shopping choices, so our annual venture had turned out to be a popular destination for others seeking seasonal costumes and decorations.

"Kids are fun," Ellie insisted.

"Sure, if you're observing them from behind security glass," I countered.

"Whatever." Ellie picked up a ghost costume and headed toward the checkout counter of the Halloween shop that had temporarily rented space on Main Street. So much for Ellie's good mood. I guess I shouldn't have teased her about the kids. I like kids. I really do. It was just that today, with half the under-ten population of Ashton Falls gathered in one small space, things were louder and much more hectic than I'm used to. Most of the time I prefer to enjoy the company of children in small doses. *Very* small doses.

"What's her deal?" Levi asked.

"I'm not sure. It seems like she's been in a bad mood all week. I know she broke up with boyfriend number seventeen. Maybe this whole marathon-dating thing she's been doing is getting to her."

After her fiancé left her to return to his hometown, where he married the mother of his two-year-old daughter, Ellie had decided she wanted a baby of her own to fill the void left by the toddler she missed more and more every day. She'd wanted to look into having a baby the no-daddy way, but I'd convinced her to wait until she had a chance to really think things through. For the past three months she'd been out on a date almost every night, but so far she'd yet to meet Mr. Right.

"So why doesn't she just quit?" Levi wondered.

"You know why."

I felt bad for the difficult situation in which my two best friends had found themselves. I was certain that each loved the other, but I was equally sure that a relationship between them could never work. Ellie was obsessed with the idea of starting a family and Levi was equally committed to the idea of waiting to have children until some point in the *very* distant future, if at all.

"So anyway, you were saying before the mini tornado blew through?" Levi prompted.

I shrugged. "I forget. I don't think it was important. I'm going to go to check on Ellie."

I set the mask I'd been holding aside and wandered to the front of the store, where I'd spied Ellie at the checkout counter. I hated to see my best friend miss out on the fun of the season. Normally, Ellie was cheerful and easygoing. I guess her obsession with everything baby was really getting to her. At first I couldn't understand where she was coming from, but now that I have a baby sister and am able to experience firsthand how sweet and adorable infants can be, I guess I'm beginning to sympathize with her situation to some degree.

"Have you seen Zak?" I asked Ellie as I walked up beside her.

"In the back, looking at life-size monsters. The guy is really in to the whole decorating thing. If you aren't careful, your lakefront mansion is going to look like the Haunted Mansion at Disneyland."

"Wouldn't that be awesome?" I grinned. I know this may be hard to believe, but my world-traveling, been-there-done-everything boyfriend had apparently never been to a Halloween party. How does anyone get to the ripe old age of twenty-five without bobbing for apples or eating snacks out of a coffin at least once in their life?

"We still need to get together to discuss the food for the party," I added. "I'm thinking theme food, like mummy dogs and eyeball skewers."

"I'm sure I can come up with something," Ellie answered with little enthusiasm.

"And I was thinking maybe we should make up goodie bags for any trick-or-treaters we might get. I have a few ideas, but you're really the queen of the gift bag, if you want to help."

"Sure, that would be fun."

Ellie's tone of voice didn't really match the words she'd spoken, and I couldn't help but notice the tears that had welled up in her eyes.

"What's wrong?" I asked.

"Nothing."

"Come on, Ellie. You've been down all week, and we both know that you usually love Halloween."

"I know, and I do love Halloween. It's just that . . ." Ellie paused. She took a deep breath as she struggle to get her emotions under control. "You know, I think I've changed my mind about the costume. I'm just going to wear something I already have. Can you put this back for me?" She handed me the ghost costume.

"Can I help?"

"I have a bit of a headache. I think I'm just going to head home."

I watched as she turned toward the side door that exited into the parking lot.

"You don't want to come to dinner with us?" I called after her. The four of us had planned to go out for pizza and beer.

"Not tonight. I'll see you tomorrow."

I watched Ellie put her head down as she hurried away. Poor Ellie was really having a tough time. As her best friend, I felt like I should be able to do something to help her. The problem was that I had no idea what that something might be.

"Ellie leave?" Levi asked as he walked up behind me with the pirate costume in his arms.

"Yeah. I guess she wasn't feeling well. She said she was going to skip dinner and catch up with us tomorrow."

Levi frowned. "I guess I'll skip dinner too."

"Are you sure? You love beer-and-pizza night."

"I know, but I don't really feel like playing a third wheel and Darla is busy. I'll catch up with you tomorrow."

"Okay. I'll see you at the game. Maybe we can do something after," I suggested.

"Yeah, that would be fun. I'm sure we'll have a victory to celebrate."

"I'm sure we will. Mulligan's at six?"

"Sounds like a plan. Darla is out of town for the entire weekend at some yoga retreat, so it will just be the four of us, assuming Ellie comes and doesn't bring one of her many-in-a-long-line of dates."

"I'll ask her, but she hasn't mentioned a date. Are you sure you don't want to come with Zak and me tonight?" I tried one last time.

"Yeah, I'm sure." Levi kissed me on the cheek. "I'll see you tomorrow."

I felt bad that my friends were going to miss out on a weekly tradition, but as I looked across the store, I realized that their defection meant that I was going to have Frankenstein all to myself.

"What do you think?" Zak asked as he walked toward me with a mask over his head.

"It's perfect."

Zak is tall. Before I stopped resenting him and starting loving him, I often referred to him as Frankenstein freakishly tall.

"Maybe I should go as the Bride of Frankenstein," I suggested.

"Did you say bride?"

"Maybe," I answered. "Although I guess I really should wait to see if Frankenstein is all freak and no show."

"Oh, I've got show," Frankenstein promised.

I couldn't see Zak's face under the mask, but I was certain he was grinning. He'd asked me to marry him last July, and as of today, I'd yet to give him an answer. I know that he knows that one day I'll take the leap and formally accept his offer, but for now, we're just getting used to each other as full-time roomies.

"Is there a costume to go with that mask?" I asked.

Zak pulled his head off. "Of course there's a costume. A really great costume. Where did the others go?"

"To pout. How about we pick up the pizza and take it home? I want to watch the John Carpenter marathon that's on tonight."

Zak grabbed a shopping cart from the front of the store. "Sound good to me. I could go for some classic horror, but I need to pick up a few things I found for the house."

"More monsters?"

"You can never have too many monsters," Zak reminded me. "Or lights," he added as he tossed at least twenty boxes of orange twinkle lights in the basket.

"It's a good thing we don't have neighbors. You have enough lights to land a plane."

Zak filled two carts in record time. I had to admit that the house was going to look awesome. Zak had even picked up an orange light for the pool so that it would glow with Halloween colors, although I doubted anyone would be swimming. The pool was heated, but there was a definite crispness to the air as the long days of summer waned toward the short days of winter.

"I've been thinking about the mailbox." Zak paused to consider a display of mechanical decorations.

"The mailbox?"

"Maybe we should rig it so that a hand reaches out at you when you open the door on the front."

"Our mailman is seventy-two years old. You wouldn't want to give Mr. Hanover a heart attack, would you?"

"No, I guess not." Zak returned the mechanical arm to the pile. "I thought Mr. Hanover was asked to retire."

"He was, but after sitting through the speech the mayor prepared, he politely thanked them for their concern and then promised to be at work bright and early the next morning. They even tried hiring someone else, but Mr. Hanover just showed up all that much earlier the next day, picked up the mail before the new guy arrived, and then went out on his route as usual."

"I suppose they could change the locks on the outer door of the post office."

"Yeah, I suppose they could, but I don't think anyone *really* wants to see Mr. Hanover retire. He's been doing that same route since before my dad was born. I did hear that he agreed to start training an assistant, so you might have someone younger to scare the begeebees out of next year."

Zak smiled.

I decided to get into the long line while Zak finished gathering his supplies. At the rate the line was moving, it would be breakfast before it was our turn to check out. As I looked around at the overstimulated children running up and down the aisles, I thought fondly of my own Halloweens as a child. My dad always dressed up in a gory costume when he took me trick-or-treating. Some years Ellie and Levi would come with us, but there were a few years when it was just the two of us running from house to house so that I could hit as many as possible in the hours between 6 and 9 p.m.

I was nearing the front of the line, so I was looking around the store for Zak when I noticed a man wearing a dark overcoat and a fedora. His attire seemed odd for this decade, so I couldn't help but watch as he walked slowly up and down each aisle without stopping to look at anything in particular. If I had to guess, he was looking for some*one* rather than some*thing*.

"Do you see that guy in the overcoat?" I asked as Zak walked up beside me. I tried not to cringe as Zak pushed the two heaping carts of Halloween decorations into line. Ellie was right: At the rate Zak was going, our house was going to look like a magical theme park ride.

"The guy walking around aimlessly?" Zak clarified.

"Yeah. He's acting strange. Do you recognize him?"

"No. He doesn't look familiar. Maybe he's a visitor?"

"Maybe. It's just that my Zodar is tingling."

Now that I'd solved a total of eight murders in the past year, my friends had started teasing me about having some sort of Zoe Radar—or Zodar for short—when it came to both murder victims and murder suspects. I had to wonder which I was sensing.

"Maybe your Zodar is on the fritz. No one is dead," Zak pointed out.

"Yet," I replied.

# Chapter 2

## Saturday, October 18

Sometimes I really hate being right.

The day started off okay. Zak and I slept in, had a nice brunch on the deck overlooking the lake, then spent the rest of the morning putting out the decorations Zak had bought the previous evening. By the time we headed into town to Levi's game, the house looked like a Hollywood movie set. Once we arrived at the football field, Zak, an unpaid and unofficial assistant coach of sorts, joined Levi on the sidelines and I met up with Ellie in the stands.

"The team looks good," Ellie commented as we scored our third touchdown, bringing the score to 21–7. Ellie had taken a bit more care with her outfit today, topping soft suede pants in a light fawn color with a fuzzy orange sweater that accentuated her figure perfectly. I hoped the attention to her appearance meant that she was finally working her way out of the funk she'd been in for the past week.

"I'm glad you decided to come," I said. "It seems like we've both been so busy lately that we haven't had much of a chance to hang out, just the two of us. I love living with Zak, but I really miss us."

"Yeah, me too." Ellie smiled and squeezed my hand, but I could see that her smile didn't quite reach her eyes. "I guess I have been pretty busy with work, dating, and the Haunted Hamlet. When I volunteered to be chairperson for the event, I had no idea I'd be so busy with everything else."

"How can I help?"

"I guess if you have time, it would be a huge help if you met Joel at the Henderson house this afternoon while I meet with the food vendors."

"The Henderson house?" I paled.

For a number of years Joel had overseen the spookification of the haunted barn, one of the many features of Haunted Hamlet, our annual fall fund-raiser. This year the barn we normally used was unavailable, so the committee had decided to look for an equally eerie venue. After a bit of discussion, the committee voted to hold the event in a barn that shared the same piece of property as a house many believe to be an *actual* haunted house.

"I guess he's been working on setting up the props in the haunted barn and wanted to go over a few ideas with someone from the committee. Initially, I told him that I'd meet him after the game, but the man from the catering company who's overseeing the food for this year's event needs to meet with me today as well. I was going to call Joel and reschedule, but if you don't mind covering for me, we can get both men taken care of today, so hopefully I won't have to deal with the Hamlet tomorrow."

"Yeah, okay, I'll meet with Joel," I agreed as our team intercepted the ball and everyone in the stands jumped to their feet. "Did you see that catch?" I cheered.

"I think this puts David in the lead for most interceptions in the state," Ellie commented as the crowd went wild.

"He's really something," I agreed. "I heard that our little town might even get a visit from some college scouts this year, given David's numbers coupled with our strong showing in the state championship last year."

"David has a real shot at the pros. I hope it works out for him."

The next play resulted in a touchdown, bringing the score to 28–7, with the Bulldogs pulling into a comfortable lead.

"What time do I need to meet Joel?" I asked after we kicked off the ball and the Juniper Valley Titans took the offense.

"I told him someone would meet him before five. He indicated that he would be working in the barn until dark, so it made sense to meet with him after the game. I'll text the food vendor and let him know that I can meet him as he requested. I'm hoping we can both be done in time to meet up at Mulligan's at six as we discussed."

"Sounds like a plan. I know I've scarfed down both a hot dog and an order of nachos since we've been sitting here, but I really am starving."

"I guess you've burned off the food you've eaten with all the jumping around you've been doing. By the way, I love your jersey. It looks just like the guys'. Where did you get it?" Ellie asked.

"Levi gave it to me. It was too small for anyone on the team, so he asked me if I wanted it, and of course I did."

"I should see if he has another one that I can wear when we play Bryton Lake in two weeks," Ellie commented.

"Bryton Lake played last night and won, so if we win today, which it looks like we will, both teams will be undefeated. It should be a good game, but I think we have the advantage this year."

"Yeah. I just hope we don't have the same pregame shenanigans that got Levi arrested last year."

"You and me both."

By the time the final buzzer sounded, the Ashton Falls Bulldogs had beat the Juniper Valley Titans by a score of 38–14. Zak decided to stay to help Levi with the postgame meeting, so I took Zak's truck and headed to the Henderson house on my own.

I was less than thrilled about the committee's choice of venue for this year's haunted barn. Not only had I found an *actual* dead body in the house the previous October, but the Henderson house has given me major willies since I was a little girl. Still, I didn't want to appear to be a scaredy-cat in front of Zak or anyone else, so when Levi asked Zak to stay for the team meeting, I bravely assured everyone that I was fine meeting with Joel on my own, and that it was no problem at all for me to meet up with them at Mulligan's later that evening.

According to local legend, the previous owner of the house, Hezekiah Henderson, was a crazed lunatic in life and, by all accounts, a crazed ghost in death. Hezekiah had been an old man already when I was a child. Although he seemed to have adequate financial resources to do whatever it was he wanted, what he chose to do was to live as a recluse who rarely if ever left his creepy old house. When I was seven, one of my classmates told me that, in his youth, Hezekiah had murdered and then dismembered over a hundred people. It was rumored that he buried the body parts under the floorboards in the basement and then settled into a life of seclusion in order to maintain the spell he'd used to trap the souls of his victims in a sort of limbo for all time.

As I parked in front of the house, I reminded myself that the story couldn't possibly be true. If Hezekiah *had* murdered a hundred people, he surely would have been arrested, and even if he'd managed to avoid incarceration due to some powerful black magic, as many of the kids in town believed, the spell would have been broken and the souls released the moment the old man finally died. As with many local legends, no one in town will admit to actually believing the strange tale, but when Hezekiah died and a distant heir tried to sell the property, no one would buy it at any price. As a result, the house has stood empty for more than fifteen years.

"Joel," I called as I walked slowly toward the front of the barn. The barn was large and in much better repair than the house, and Joel had already started to install the mechanical props he used to scare people year after year.

"Are you in here?" I called again when no one answered.

I took a few steps inside and looked around. It was evident by the equipment lying around that he had been there recently. I decided to return to the truck and call Ellie. Maybe she'd gotten her times messed up. Joel didn't appear to be on the property, and I didn't see his truck, but it was odd that the door to the barn stood wide open. I knew from previous discussions with Joel that his props were worth a lot of money.

I glanced at the house as I made my way back to the truck. The building gave me the creeps. It's not that I believe in ghosts exactly, but even the most stalwart nonbeliever would have to admit that in the fifteen years the house has been empty, strange and inexplicable occurrences have taken place within its walls. Hezekiah died when I was nine. When I was twelve, a group of counselors from a nearby summer camp had snuck into the house to party away from the watchful eye of the camp administrator. I don't remember everything that happened, but by the end of that terrible night, three people were dead and one was missing.

For several years after that, no one had dared enter the creepy structure, but as time went by the rumors ceased, and homeless vagrants began to use the building to ward off cold winter nights. The legend of Hezekiah Henderson and the haunted basement faded and became dormant until I was fifteen, when three homeless men had been found dead from no apparent cause other than fear-induced heart failure.

When I was seventeen, a group of kids prowling the streets late at night had reported hearing the sound of crying from within the house's dark walls, and when I was twenty, something that looked a lot like blood appeared on the back exterior wall. According to the authorities, these incidents, as well as several others, had logical and scientific explanations, although no one has actually revealed what those might be. Most accept the vague answers they've been given, but there are others of us who wonder if, perhaps, the house really is haunted.

After returning to the truck, I called Ellie to let her know that Joel had apparently left early.

"Hey, Zoe. How'd the meeting go?" Ellie asked.

"It didn't. Joel must have left early. I looked around in the barn, but he was nowhere to be found."

"That's odd. I just talked to him this morning and he said he'd be there until dark."

"I guess something came up, although it's strange that he left the barn door open."

"Hang on while I check my messages. Maybe he called while I was talking to the food vendor."

Ellie put me on hold. A lone rain cloud drifted across the sky, blocking what was left of the sun. I took the phone from my ear and held it at my side, looking toward the front of the house, where a black cat was pacing back and forth in front of the door. She was far enough away that I couldn't see her clearly so I couldn't be certain, but it looked like she might have recently had kittens.

"Zoe, are you there?" I heard Ellie come back on the line.

I returned the phone to my ear. "Yeah, I'm here. Did Joel call?"

"Yeah, he did. I'm sorry I didn't notice he'd called before you went all the way out there. He cut his hand, so he headed home early. I called him to arrange for a reschedule, and he asked if you would mind locking the barn. He said he meant to go back and do it but got tied up. There's a combination lock on the door. You'll need to unlock the mechanism and then relock it after the door is closed. Joel gave me the number; I can read it to you over the phone."

"Yeah, okay. I can head back over to the barn and lock up, but give me a few minutes." I began walking toward the cat.

"Why? What's going on?"

"There's a cat on the porch who looks like she's trying to get into the house. I'm going to check her out. I can call you back if you'd like."

"No, that's okay. I can wait on the line."

I put my phone on hold and jogged over to the cat. I bent down and petted the friendly cat, who immediately began purring. "Did you get locked out?" I wondered. It was obvious by her swollen nipples that she had recently had kittens. The cat meowed and rubbed against my leg. I couldn't help but notice the look of despair on her delicate face. Poor baby must be frantic that she had become separated from her babies. She must have gone out when the door was open and then been unable to get back in.

I clicked back on the line. "The cat looks like she's had kittens recently," I informed Ellie. "My guess is that the babies are inside, but Mama got locked out. I'm going to go in and see if I can find the kittens. If I bring them to the Zoo, they'll have a much better chance of making it to adulthood than they will on their own."

"You're going into that spooky old house alone? You do remember what happened the last time?"

"Yeah, I remember," I answered. "Just stay on the line as backup and I'll be fine."

"Yeah, 'cause that worked so well before."

"The last time there was a body in the basement. What are the odds of that happening again?"

"Knowing you? Pretty good."

"I'll be fine. If you hear me being ax-murdered, call Salinger," I said.

"You do realize you're insane?"

"Yeah, so I've been told."

I gathered my courage and opened the front door of the musty old house. There were decorations stacked in the living room, which led me to believe that Joel must have been using the house as a staging area to assemble his props before installing them in the barn. I imagine that was how the cat got out. Joel probably left the door open while going back and forth between the two structures and then closed it when he left.

The house was murky and dusty, with cobwebs hanging from every corner. After old Hezekiah died, the house had been boarded up with all of his furniture and personal possessions inside. Over the years, many of the items had been stolen, but rotting furniture, including a sofa and several chairs, still remained. Many of the walls were covered in graffiti, and the dust on the floor was so thick that you couldn't make out the original color of the wood.

The cat seemed to be waiting for me to follow her, so I headed toward the hallway, where she stood. I paused as something crashed overhead.

"What's that noise?" Ellie whispered.

"I'm not sure." It sounded like someone was walking around upstairs.

"You should get out of there while you still can," Ellie warned.

"I'm fine. It was probably just the wind blowing in through an open window. I really want to find the kittens."

"Do you see the mother cat?"

"Yeah, she's heading down the hall. I think she wants me to follow her."

I began walking in the direction the cat seemed to be leading. She stopped and turned around every few feet, as if to ensure that I was following. If I had to guess, she hadn't been on her own for long and welcomed the help that she somehow knew I was willing to provide.

"Maybe you should just go back tomorrow during the day. I really don't like the idea of you poking around in there by yourself when it's getting dark. Weird stuff happens in that house after dark."

"I'll be fine," I assured her as I headed down a narrow hallway. "I really want to get the cat and her babies to safety. She looks overwhelmed."

"She's a cat. I doubt cats get 'overwhelmed.'"

"Obviously you've never had a cat."

"Maybe not, but we both know that you tend to attribute human emotion to animals. I'm sure the cat is fine, but I'm not sure you will be if you wander around that rickety old place at night."

"It's twilight, not night," I pointed out.

I followed the black cat toward the back of the house. Most of the rooms were bedrooms, covered in dust and cobwebs. Many still possessed the furniture that must have belonged to Hezekiah Henderson, while others likely had been stripped bare by vandals.

"She's headed to the basement," I informed Ellie. "She just went down the stairs."

"Zoe Donovan, if you find another body, I am never going to speak to you again."

"Don't worry; I'll be fine." I walked slowly down the steps to the basement and let out a short scream as I opened the door.

"What's wrong?" Ellie demanded.

"It's okay." I took a deep breath as my heart rate slowed back to a normal rhythm. "It was just a rat."

"Do you see anything?" Ellie asked.

I looked around. "Not so far. I'm going to check the back of the room."

I tried to convince myself that there was nothing to worry about in spite of the murky shadows and scurrying sounds all around me. I'd pretty much convinced myself that the feeling of being watched was all in my imagination until I saw a pile of old sheets shaped suspiciously like a body. I was about to tell Ellie to call 911 when the body in the sheets moved and I passed out cold on the dusty floor of Hezekiah Henderson's house of horrors.

"So it was just a sheet full of old rags." Levi laughed as I told him the story.

"It was humiliating and not at all funny," I said with a groan as I looked around Mulligan's Bar and Grill to make sure no one was listening in on our conversation. Several patrons were sitting at the bar carving pumpkins for the annual contest, while "Monster Mash" played in the background. It appeared as if the occupants of the bar were busy listening to the music or involved in their own conversations, which was good, because the last thing I wanted was for anyone to find out what a fool I'd made of myself.

I, super sleuth Zoe Donovan, had not only passed out when I saw the bundle I believed to be a body move, but Ellie had called Sheriff Salinger in a panic when I didn't answer her repeated attempts to make sure I was okay. Salinger then sent all four members of the Aston Falls Sheriff's Department to the house to rescue me. By the time they showed up and determined that I hadn't fallen victim to a poltergeist on a rampage, Zak, Ellie, and Levi had shown up as well, so we decided to go out for a bite to eat as planned.

"Maybe it was a ghostly pile of rags," Levi teased.

"Bite me."

"Leave Zoe alone." Ellie kicked Levi. "The mind can play tricks on us during times of stress."

"I've never been so humiliated," I complained.

Zak just looked at me.

"Okay, I've never been so humiliated *recently.*"

"Define recently." Levi was still laughing.

"Okay, I've never been more humiliated this month."

Let's face it, I'm known to be something of a loose cannon when it comes to getting myself into embarrassing situations. It's not that I'm careless exactly. It's more that I tend to power my way through life with my enthusiasm leading the way and my common sense trailing along at a distant pace. I couldn't help but feel bad that I'd lost track of the mama cat and failed to find the kittens. It was going to get cold tonight, and I hated to think of them all alone in that creepy old house.

Zak squeezed my hand. "She'll be fine until tomorrow," he offered as he apparently read my mind.

"I know. I just feel like I let her down. She seemed to be leading me to the kittens and then she just disappeared. It was dark in the basement. I guess she must have stashed her babies toward the back of the room, out of the way. I don't even know if she had food and water."

"Do you want to go back now?" Zak asked.

Actually, I did.

"Are you crazy? It's pitch-black out," Ellie said. "The cat will be fine."

"We have flashlights," I said in what I hoped was a persuasive voice. "And there are four of us, and you know what they say about safety in numbers."

"That sounds like the opening line of every horror movie I've ever seen," Ellie pointed out.

"I'll just pop in, get the cat and kittens, and pop out. You can wait in the truck if you want," I offered.

"Alone? No thanks. Besides, if the cat and her kittens were in the basement, don't you think Salinger and his men would have seen them when they showed up to rescue you? Don't you think you would have seen them when you came to? Chances are the kittens, if they're even in the house, are in a different room entirely."

"Good point," I had to admit. "Salinger hurried me out of the house, but I did have a chance to look around the room a bit and it was completely empty except for the rags. I wonder where she could have gone."

"After you blacked out, she probably left the basement the same way she entered," Levi theorized.

"Let's face it: that house is huge. You'll never find the cat in the dark. You should do as Zak suggested and go back tomorrow," Ellie directed.

"Yeah, I guess you're right. I'm sure the kittens will be fine one more night."

The problem was that even as I said the words, I didn't really believe them. I know that it was crazy to worry about the cat and her offspring. Ellie was probably correct and they were fine. As Zak drove us toward his lakefront home, I began to worry that the cat might have gotten out again when Salinger and his men were responding to my false alarm. I hated to think what would happen to the babies if they were separated from their mom overnight.

"You want to go back tonight, don't you?" Zak asked as we pulled off the main highway onto the road that led down to the lake and our home.

"I really do," I admitted. "I know it's dark, but it's only seven thirty. It's not exactly the witching hour."

Zak pulled over to the side of the road and then executed a perfect U-turn.

"You think I'm crazy."

Zak smiled. "Maybe a little, but I love that about you. In all the time we've been dating, I've never been bored."

"I just can't seem to get the cat off my mind. I know Ellie doesn't think cats can become overwhelmed, but she really did seem stressed. My guess is that she's a recent stray and this is her first litter."

"Don't worry; we'll find her. If she led you toward the basement, then she's most likely still in the basement, so we'll look there first."

"Thanks. I'll owe you."

Zak grinned. "I like it when you owe me."

"Yeah, I bet you do." I grinned back.

If the Henderson house was frightening by day, it was downright terrifying at night. At least I had Zak and the largest flashlight I could find with me this time. Two-storied, with an attic, it sits toward the back of a large, overgrown lot surrounded by an iron fence and an impenetrable gate that opens onto a dirt drive leading to a walkway comprised of four rotted steps and an equally rotted porch.

I began calling for the cat as soon as Zak and I entered the house. I was certain the kittens would be found in the basement, but I could hear movement coming from the second floor. I followed closely behind Zak as we slowly climbed the stairs. He stopped abruptly as he came to the top.

"What is it?" I asked.

"You'd better call Salinger. It looks like your Zodar wasn't on the fritz after all."

# Chapter 3

## Sunday, October 19

"The monsters look awesome," I commented as I walked in through the front door of the house Zak and I now shared carrying takeout bags filled with sandwiches and salads the following afternoon. Ellie had been experimenting with new menu items and had called to ask if I was interested in taking home some of her test subjects. Of course I was. I'm always up for free food, especially when it's something Ellie whipped up in her magical kitchen.

Charlie and Bella trotted up to meet me while Marlow meowed at me from the top of the stairs, though Spade was nowhere to be seen. Spade has always been the sort that preferred his own company to that of others, so I wasn't overly surprised that he seemed to disappear more often than not in Zak's huge house. If I had to guess, I'd be willing to bet that he was in Zak's office, watching the fish in the 500-gallon saltwater aquarium Zak installed after our trip to Maui. Lying on the back of Zak's leather sofa had become his favorite napping spot.

"I've been thinking about the overall impression of the house our guests will experience when they head into the drive. I think the lights are great, but if we really want to pull off the party of the decade, we need a lot more animation." Zak's eyes lit up when he said the last word.

"Animation?"

"Yeah. Things that move and jump out at you. What they offer in town is pretty limited, but I've spent some time on the Internet, and I think I've come up with a visual display that's going to blow everyone away."

Even I found Zak's obsession with this party odd. For years he'd traveled the world, not owning much of anything. In the year since he'd bought this house, he'd accumulated quite a bit of stuff, but the degree to which he was Halloween crazy seemed to be proportionately out of character.

"You ordered this stuff already?"

Zak nodded. "Overnight mail. It'll be here tomorrow."

"Great," I said with more enthusiasm than I felt.

Don't get me wrong; like I said, I love Halloween. I just didn't want Zak to be let down if everything didn't come together the way he'd imagined. I usually go overboard with grandiose expectations, while Zak is the levelheaded one. Had we somehow switched roles when we moved in together?

"I'm excited to see what you've planned," I said, like the awesome girlfriend I am.

I recently took one of those quizzes in a women's magazine that was supposed to tell you what kind of a girlfriend you were. The questions were ridiculous and seemed to have nothing to do with relationships; still, I was expecting to find out that I was the "Perfect Girlfriend," or a "Best-Friend Girlfriend." What I wasn't expecting was to be labeled a "Self-Centered Girlfriend." I mean, really, how can you tell what kind of a girlfriend a person is by asking them what kind of music they listen to, what their favorite color is, what type of flower they prefer, or, among other equally ridiculous questions, what they considered to be the perfect date?

I don't put a lot of stock in these kinds of quizzes and more often than not simply laugh off the results, but somehow after learning my result, I found that I wanted to be a more giving and supportive girlfriend.

"I was thinking that we could go to that traveling opera that's going to be coming to the Bryton Lake Community Theater next month," I said as I attempted to score another point in the Best Girlfriend *Ever* category.

"You hate opera," Zak pointed out.

"I suppose it isn't my favorite thing, but I want to do something you'd enjoy." I smiled sweetly.

"I see." Zak grinned. "I don't suppose you took that quiz in the magazine you left on the coffee table."

"How'd you know?"

"You circled your answers."

Zak came over and wrapped his arms around me. "Just so you know, I think the only reason you weren't happy with your answer is because the stupid quiz didn't even have the right answer as an option."

"Oh, and what would that be?"

*Please don't say The Big Ol' Mess Girlfriend with commitment issues and a tendency toward jealousy*, I thought to myself.

"The right answer would be," Zak kissed the tip of my nose, "the perfectly original girlfriend who has a compassionate heart and a strong spirit that I am madly in love with and want to spend the rest of my life with."

"Oh." I hugged him. "You're the best boyfriend. I don't deserve you."

"I think you do, but if you want to do something you think I'd enjoy, I'm pretty sure it's not the opera."

I smiled as Zak grinned at me. I love that he can't seem to keep his hands off me in spite of the fact that we're now living together.

"Later," I promised. "For now, I want to know if you found out anything about the victim in the Henderson house while I was in town."

Zak kissed me firmly on the lips and then took a step back. "Let's eat and I'll fill you in."

It was warm for October, so we took our food out to the deck. There are October days in Ashton Falls when the weather is simply perfect: clear sky, blue lake, no wind, warm temperatures. Today was one of those perfect autumn days. I unwrapped the crab sandwich Ellie had insisted I try and gave half to Zak.

"This is wonderful," I said after taking a bite so large my mouth could barely contain the wonderful combination of flavors.

"It's got a kick, but not so much as to make it unbearably hot. I like it," Zak agreed.

"The pasta salad Ellie sent looks really good as well." I peeled off the lid and handed Zak a fork. "When she said she added some pasta salad to our bag I was picturing something heavy, but this is actually refreshing. So fill me in on what you found while I was out."

The previous night we had not only found the mama cat and her four newborn kittens, all of which were tucked safely away in one of our spare bedrooms, but also the body of the man we'd noticed in the costume shop on Friday evening. He was lying at the bottom of the stairs that led from the second floor to the attic. It looked as if he had simply fallen and broken his neck as he attempted to access the attic via the steep, narrow staircase. Salinger didn't suspect foul play, but I wasn't so certain.

Zak picked up a napkin and wiped his mouth before speaking. "The victim's name is Adam Davenport. He was a scholar, writer, and filmmaker. He came to Ashton Falls two weeks ago to film a documentary about paranormal activity in this area."

I swallowed and set my sandwich down. "You're kidding. The guy was a ghost hunter?"

Except for the fact that a man was dead, which was always a tragic thing, the setup was too good to be true: a ghost hunter falls victim to the spooks he's studying right before Halloween. Talk about a perfect plot for a cheesy movie.

"I'm not sure if 'ghost hunter' is exactly the right term, but according to what I've been able to find, the man was a legit ghost researcher. He had a doctorate in consciousness studies from a major university and was widely respected in his field."

"Consciousness studies?"

"It's a field of study that focuses on moving toward an integrated understanding of human consciousness by bringing together differing fields, including philosophy, neuroscience, medicine, and the physical sciences. I know it sounds pretty out there, but there are accredited colleges that offer postgraduate work in the field."

"So why was he here? In Ashton Falls?"

"To study the Henderson house. He wrote a paper about six months ago chronicling the paranormal activity in the house and came to the area to prove or disprove the presence of paranormal beings."

"Okay, so this guy is in town to study paranormal activity in a house where weird stuff has been happening for years and mysteriously falls down the stairs. Seems like a pretty big coincidence."

"Yeah, I have to agree."

"Have you informed Salinger about the man's profession?" I asked.

"I did. He'd already discovered most of what I found on the Web."

"And does he suspect a supernatural cause for the man's death?" I wondered.

"He does not."

"But we're thinking there could be something more going on?" I fished.

"It does seem like the circumstances leading up to his death point to something more," Zak agreed.

"So you think he was killed by a poltergeist," I added.

I could tell by the skeptical look on Zak's face that of the two of us, I was the *only* one who believed that our suspect might just possibly be living impaired.

After lunch, Zak and I attended an emergency meeting of the events committee. Joel's haunted barn was the cornerstone of the five-day event, but Salinger had closed off access to the Henderson property, which meant we were once again without a venue for the most popular event of the Haunted Hamlet. Without it, it was doubtful that we'd be able to attract the visitors we needed to make the fund-raiser a success. Given the fact that the meeting was unplanned, only half of the committee members were able to make it on such short notice, but Zak came with me, bringing the total to seven. Normally, event committee meetings were held in the back room of Rosie's Café, but since today was a Sunday, Rosie's was packed. Hazel Hampton, our town librarian, was off for the day and offered her spacious living room as a substitute.

Unlike the house I share with Zak, which is decked out with every spooky decoration imaginable, Hazel had decorated her home tastefully with fall accents depicting the season rather than the holiday. The dining table was covered with a cloth in burnt orange that was accented by a vase of yellow, orange, red, and dark purple flowers, which I suspected had been clipped from her garden. As was her custom, Hazel had set out an arrangement of yummy treats, including my favorite pumpkin cookies, to go with the coffee and fruit punch she provided.

As I mingled with the other members of the committee, waiting for the stragglers to arrive, I could sense the elevated level of tension that seemed to consist of both concern and excitement at the same time. I supposed that the others felt much as I did. While I was concerned that the annual event would be a bust if we couldn't figure out an alternative to the haunted barn, knowing that a parapsychologist had died in a house everyone suspected was haunted just days before the annual Haunted Hamlet gave an extra feeling of awesomeness to the event. Okay, I guess that sounds insensitive and morbid. I don't mean to indicate that I'm taking a casual view of death, but there's something about the holiday that makes spooky and unexplained sort of cool, and it wasn't as if I'd ever actually met Adam Davenport.

"It looks like we're all here," Hazel said, calling those of us who had wandered outside into the house.

Zak and I went back inside, where we joined Hazel, Willa Walton, Gilda Reynolds, my dad—Hank Donovan—Levi, and Joel. Ellie and Paul Iverson had to work, and Tawny Upton was home with her kids.

"I assume we all know and understand the situation presented by the events of the past twenty-four hours," Willa began. "While I am saddened by the death of the man visiting our town, I feel that as the event committee, we should address the problem at hand. The Haunted Hamlet is set to open Thursday afternoon. That gives us exactly four days to find another venue in which to hold the haunted barn."

"I've been setting up for a week," Joel informed the group. "It's too late to start over, even if we find another location."

"Maybe we should forget about the haunted barn and go in a different direction entirely," I suggested.

"A Haunted Hamlet without a haunted barn?" Hazel gasped. "The haunted barn is and always has been the cornerstone of the event."

"I realize that," I began, "but I really don't see what choice we have. We still have the zombie run, the kiddie carnival, and the spooky maze, as well as the pumpkin patch and pumpkin-carving competition. Maybe that will be enough."

"The Haunted Hamlet is a huge revenue source for us," Willa worried. "If we can't attract folks from the valley, we might be forced to cut programs next year. We're already projecting a huge deficit. As we've discussed in previous meetings, the only way to meet the needs of emergency services will be to cut funding to the arts. If we don't have a good showing this holiday season, we might not be able to fund programs such as subsidized day care, summer youth camp, or theater at any level."

"Okay, so what can we do to replace the haunted barn that wouldn't require a lot of props or preparation?" Hazel asked.

"I've always thought that having both the haunted barn and the spooky maze was sort of redundant," I offered. "Maybe we can come up with something totally different that might even draw a slightly different crowd."

"What about a play?" Willa looked at Gilda, who ran the local theater arts program.

"Not enough time," she responded. "Although doing a play next year would be a wonderful idea."

"What about a movie?" Zak suggested.

"What kind of movie?" Hazel asked.

"I have a friend who works in Hollywood and might be able to get us the rights to show some of the old classics like *Dracula* or *The Blob*. We could have the drama club dress up and maybe show up at key points in the film to add a sense of eeriness to the event."

"I once attended a showing of *The Rocky Horror Picture Show* where they had people who acted out parts of the movie," Levi offered.

"We have four days," I reminded everyone.

"What about a hayride?" Gilda suggested. "I know several people who have hay wagons, and the forest provides a naturally spooky landscape. We can write a script and get a couple of my better students to narrate it as the wagons travel along a designated trail. I have other actors who can dress up like ghosts and zombies and linger about in the forest for the wagon to happen across. I've already checked the weather forecast and it's supposed to be clear."

"I can set up a few props to give a hayride a spooky feel," Joel offered. "It won't be as elaborate as the haunted barn, but it will be something."

"We won't be able to accommodate the volume we did with the haunted house," Willa pointed out.

"We won't need to. The event will be more exclusive, so we can charge more. It's worth a try, unless someone has a better idea," Gilda insisted.

No one did.

"Let's see how many wagons we can round up. Gilda, go ahead and get started organizing the narrators and the actors who'll be placed in the forest."

"I'll check with Ellie, but I'd be willing to bet she'd help organize a snack bar at the staging area if we can get enough volunteers to run it. I figure there'll be folks waiting around for the next wagon, so we might as well sell them hot cider and cupcakes," I said.

"Good idea." Willa smiled at me.

"I can get the cheerleaders from Ashton Falls High School to run the snack bar at the hayride," Levi volunteered. "We could give a percentage of the proceeds directly to their camp fund."

"That's a wonderful idea," Willa responded. "The main problem I see with the idea is that, unlike the haunted barn, which we could run all day, the forest is only spooky at night, which will give us fewer hours of operation."

"True, but we can have less spooky hayrides for little kids earlier in the day," I suggested. "Sort of like they do with the spooky maze."

"Let's see what we can pull together. If you locate a wagon that will commit, call me and I'll start a list," Willa decided.

Everyone indicated their agreement as they gathered their belongings and began to disperse.

# Chapter 4

## Monday, October 20

October in Ashton Falls is a special time. Not only is the alpine village decked out in nature's grandeur as the yellow and orange of aspens paint every hillside with breathtaking color, but the downtown section of my hometown is dressed out in man-made splendor as well. As they do every year, the vendors along the main strip hang orange twinkle lights in every tree along the stretch of town that's bordered on one side by the lake and the other by the mom-and-pop shops that give my hometown its charm. Not only is every tree adorned with lights and other decorations such as handmade ghosts and rubber bats but every window is decorated as well.

While I loved all the windows along Main Street, my favorite was the miniature village Dad and Pappy set up in the window of Donovan's, the general store that has been in the family for two generations. This year Mom contributed a haunted train to the annual display that wound its way through the spooky houses, mechanical graveyard, and monster-infested swamp, so I decided to stop by and add my own piece to the magical display.

Charlie trotted over to the seating area Dad had arranged around the potbellied stove that stood in one corner of the main floor. Dad had brought all three of his dogs to work with him, so Charlie enthusiastically greeted each and every one, while Nick Benson, a retired doctor and member of the book club Pappy and I belong to, and Ethan Carlton, a retired history professor and also a book club member, focused all their energy on the game of chess they had set up on one of the tables my dad provides for just such a purpose.

"The village looks great," I commented as I kissed my dad on the cheek in greeting.

"Folks have been stopping by all week to take pictures."

"The train really does add an element of mystery," I commented. "I like the way it winds through the tunnels so that it disappears from one part of the village to reappear in another. I wanted to add my own piece to the display so I brought this."

I handed my dad a box that held a boat with a corpse sitting in it to add to the swamp.

"How did you get that fog affect over the swamp?" I asked.

"Dry ice," Dad replied.

"It's really awesome."

"Your boat goes perfectly with the rest of the scene." Dad gave me a squeeze as he placed it in the midst of the foggy landscape."

Just looking at the display gave me a feeling of warmth. Many of my most highly valued memories are of Halloween nights as a young girl, and the foggy boat scene brought up memories of summers' past as well.

"The fog over your swamp area reminds me of that summer we went camping up along the coastline of Washington State. We took the boat and spent most of our visit exploring the waterways surrounding the peninsula and the islands in the area."

Dad smiled. "And every morning a blanket of fog covered the area, making everything seem spooky and somewhat surreal," Dad offered. "I remember that trip fondly. I think it might have been one of our best."

"And spookiest," I added. "I'd just seen the original version of that movie *The Fog*, and every time the fog rolled in, I started to cry because I thought dead pirates were going to kill us. You had to wrap me up in a sleeping bag and hold me tight until I fell asleep."

Dad laughed. "I do remember that. It seems like there were two or three days when the fog came in early and I had to distract you with board games in the tent. I miss those summer camping trips we used to take, just the two of us."

"Maybe we can go camping next summer. Harper will be older, and I'm sure we can talk Mom into roughing it for a week. Zak loves to camp. He told me that he used to go all the time when he was a kid."

"Maybe instead of camping we can rent one of those cabins on the islands," Dad suggested. "It would be easier on Mom and Harper, but you and I and Zak can still take the boat out every morning. It's been a while since I've been fishing."

"Yum, fresh salmon. My mouth is watering at the thought."

"Thought of what?" Pappy joined us from the stockroom.

"Salmon," I answered. "I didn't know you were here." I kissed his wrinkled cheek.

"I was looking for those decorations we used as a display for the counter last year."

"I seem to remember packing them away in a black rubber tub. Check the storage area where we keep the Christmas decorations."

"Thanks, I think you're right."

"I was just telling Dad how great the village looks. The whole store, in fact. I really should do more at the Zoo. I hung some ghosts and bats from the ceiling and strung some orange lights around the windows, but I don't have anything to act as a main event. We had eight new kittens dropped off over the weekend, so I was going to run an ad that should bring more than your average number of locals by. It would be fun to have an awesome display."

"Maybe you should ask Zak to do a display," Dad suggested. "He really seems to enjoy the decorating aspect of the holiday."

Suddenly, I had a vision of all of our dogs barking at mechanical monsters. Still, if I had him decorate the lobby, it would bring a cozy feel to our establishment.

"Good idea," I answered after I'd taken a moment to think about it. "I'll call him when we're done here. He's helping Gilda with the display for the haunted hayride this morning. I'm betting when all is said and done, it's going to be more popular than the haunted barn."

"Have you heard anymore about the death of the ghost hunter out at the Henderson house?" Dad asked as he returned to stocking shelves.

"Not really. The crime scene guys from Bryton Lake went through the house and scoured the forest, but they didn't find anything out of the ordinary. Salinger still thinks the guy simply slipped and fell, but Zak and I aren't so sure it's as simple as that."

"The whole thing *is* really odd," Dad agreed. "Are you and Zak investigating?"

"Not as of this point. At least not officially."

"A ghost hunter dying in a haunted house seems like a setup that's exactly up your alley. Seems like you'd be all over something like this."

I shrugged. "Normally, I would, but I have the Haunted Hamlet to think about, and honestly, I have no idea what I can do that Salinger hasn't. I'm keeping my eyes and ears open. Maybe something will pop. Are you and Mom taking Harper trick-or-treating this year?"

"Your mom arranged for us to go with Jeremy and Morgan. I think Jessica and Rosalie and Ava and Jasmine may be joining us as well."

Jeremy Fisher is my assistant at Zoe's Zoo, the wild and domestic animal rescue and rehabilitation shelter I run, and Morgan is his six-month-old daughter. Harper and Morgan were born at about the same time, as was the daughter of my mom's new best friend, Ava. The fact that the three babies were so close in age created a bond of sorts between the three parents, in spite of the fact that my mom was a forty-three-year-old second-time mother, Jeremy was a twenty-one-year-old single father, and Ava was a married, twenty-eight-year-old first-time mom.

Shortly after Morgan was born, Jeremy had met blond-haired, blue-eyed Jessica Anderson and her adorable five-year-old daughter Rosalie at a bunny adoption Zoe's Zoo sponsored. Although Jessica was a bit older than Jeremy, the two had hit it off and been dating for a while now.

"Zak and I have our party on Halloween night or I'd go along. Can you stop by the house with the babies so I can get a photo?"

"I'm sure we could work that out. We plan to go early—probably around five o'clock—and then Mom and I are going to watch Morgan and Rosalie so Jeremy and Jessica can go to your shindig for a while."

"I can't wait to see the three girls dressed up for their first Halloween." I grinned. "Do you remember my first Halloween?"

"Actually, I do. Grandma made you an adorable Raggedy Ann costume and Grandma, Pappy, and I took you around to a few of our closest friends and neighbors. I have a photo in that album I kept of your first year. I really should dig it out and show Mom. She really wants to find out as much as she can about the years she missed."

"What's Harper going to be dressed as this year?" I asked.

"I have no idea. Mom is taking care of the costumes."

"Costumes? As in more than one?"

"Mom assured me that she needs a different costume for each of the various events. She mentioned something warm for the Hamlet and then something cute that you can put a coat over for trick-or-treating. Personally, I think the whole thing will be lost on a six-month-old."

"The costumes aren't for Harper; they're for Mom. She missed a lot with me and wants to be sure she experiences everything she can this time around."

"Yeah, I guess."

"Ha!" I heard Nick yell in victory from across the store. "Looks like I have checkmate again."

"Everyone gets lucky now and again," Ethan countered. The men, although good friends, engaged in a lively rivalry.

"When did you get here?" Nick asked as he looked up from the game and noticed me for the first time.

"Hours ago," I teased. Talk about tunnel vision.

"Any news about the ghost hunter?" Ethan asked.

Apparently, he hadn't heard any part of the conversation Dad and I had just shared.

"Not really. You worked in academia for most of your life: have you ever heard of an accredited college providing a degree in consciousness studies?"

"I have. The University of Edinburgh is one of the top universities in the world, and they have a whole unit dedicated to the subject. It's named the Koestler Parapsychology Unit, after the late Arthur Koestler, a student in the field."

"And the students actually hunt for ghosts?" I asked.

"I think the department focuses more on an understanding of parapsychology and the existence of psychic ability than ghost busting, but it's an interesting field of study."

"So this Davenport guy was the real deal?"

"It would appear so."

"Trenton told me that he had lunch with the man last week. Perhaps you should talk to him if you're interested in what Professor Davenport was doing at the Henderson house," Ethan offered.

Trenton Field was a psychologist and the newest member of our book club.

"Thanks. I'll call him today. It would be interesting to find out exactly what it was Mr. Davenport hoped to find—or possibly did find—before he died."

"I didn't speak to Trenton in depth about it, but he indicated that Davenport seemed to have gathered some credible data that he hoped to publish in a trade magazine. It's a shame we may never know what exactly it was he discovered."

"Maybe he took good notes that can be pulled together by someone else," I suggested.

"Maybe. So how are things looking for the hayride?" Nick asked.

"Really good, considering we just started working on it," I said. "Willa has already tracked down six wagons for a total seating capacity of sixty passengers. We figure the route should take forty minutes, with an additional ten minutes on either end to load and unload, so we're planning to run five tours on Friday night and five on Saturday, plus a kiddie tour each evening before dark. We may not net quite as much revenue as we did with the haunted house, which accommodated several thousand guests over the long weekend, but the event should go a long way toward making up the deficit created by not being able to do the house this year."

"I gave Willa the name of a man I know in the valley who has a twenty-passenger wagon. If she can arrange to have it brought up the mountain, you'll be able to carry eighty people per tour."

"That's great; thanks, Nick." I looked at the clock. "Having to come up with an alternate event to the haunted barn may turn out to be a blessing in disguise. It seems like everyone is really excited about it. Maybe we should add it to the Haunted Hamlet on a permanent basis."

"Except for the weather factor," Pappy pointed out. "It's unseasonably warm and dry this year, but I can think of quite a few Halloweens when we've had snow. At times, a lot of it."

"I see your point. We've had to cancel the haunted maze a few times, and I remember when I was six or seven, the snowbanks were as tall as I was. It was freezing outside, but Dad bundled me up and took me out anyway."

"I think we might want to stay away from adding another outdoor event," Nick agreed.

"Gilda seemed interested in doing a Halloween play, so maybe we can add that to the menu next year."

"A play would be fun," Ethan joined in. "Maybe a comedic spoof of a horror favorite like *Young Frankenstein* or *Scary Movie*."

"Or maybe a classic whodunit," Nick countered.

"I've always thought one of those audience-participation murder mysteries would be fun," Pappy added.

"Gilda is good at coming up with entertaining scripts. I'm sure we'll find just the right production." I looked at my watch. "I really should get going. We're expecting the arrival of a mountain lion from up north later this morning, so I should head over to the Zoo to make sure Jeremy has everything ready. I'll see you both at book club?"

"Definitely. *The Shining* is one of my favorite seasonal reads," Nick offered.

So far I hadn't had the time to read page one, little alone get caught up in the story. "If I don't get some free time, I may have to just watch the movie."

"That'd be cheating." Pappy chuckled.

"Yeah, well, I hate to admit it, but it wouldn't be the first time I watched the movie rather than reading the book. Unlike the three of you, I'm not retired with unlimited amounts of time on my hands."

"Hazel works and she manages to get the books read," Pappy reminded me.

"Hazel is a librarian. It's her job to read. I'm always running around, which makes it difficult to set aside time to read. I do love attending the book-club meetings and hanging out with all of you, so one way or the other, I plan to show up and participate. I'll see you on Thursday."

"Actually, we changed to Wednesday this week due to the Hamlet," Ethan reminded us.

"Okay, then, I'll see you on Wednesday."

I kissed Dad and Pappy good-bye, then headed back through town toward the Zoo. It looked like it was going to be a feline sort of week. Not only were we expecting the mountain lion but we had eight black kittens that had been dropped off from two different litters. What were the odds? I guess the Halloween spirit was alive in more ways than one.

# Chapter 5

## Tuesday, October 21

When Ellie didn't show up for the events committee meeting Tuesday morning, I decided to go over to the Beach Hut, the lakeside sandwich shop she owns, to check in on her before I headed to the Zoo. Although she'd had moments of what seemed like happiness over the weekend, overall she'd been in a funk for more than a week, and I was beginning to get concerned. I hadn't spoken to her since Saturday, which in and of itself wasn't all that odd, though normally, with everything that was going on, she'd be right there next to me in the thick of things.

"Is Ellie around?" I asked her assistant, Kelly Arlington. Ellie had hired Kelly as a waitress shortly after she opened the lakeside restaurant but had quickly promoted her to assistant once she realized how efficient she was. Kelly seemed to enjoy her job and had proved to be more than capable of running things in Ellie's absence.

"No, she called in sick. In fact, I haven't seen her for several days. She didn't even show up for our regularly scheduled weekly meeting yesterday."

I frowned. "Did she say what was wrong?"

"No, but she's been acting odd since her doctor's appointment last week," Kelly informed me. "She seemed fine before she went, but she never came back to the Beach Hut afterward. She called and said she was taking the day off and really hasn't seemed at all like herself ever since. I'm really getting worried about her. I even thought about calling you if she didn't come in today, but here you are, saving me the trouble."

"I'm going to head over to the boathouse," I decided.

"Call me after you talk to her."

"I will." I could see Kelly was really concerned and now, suddenly, I was as well. It wasn't like her to blow off the business she cared about simply because her life wasn't perfectly on track. Maybe she really was sick.

I was glad to see that Ellie's car was parked in its usual spot in front of the boathouse. Charlie began wagging his tail as he recognized his old home. I let him out the side door and waited for him to sniff around, rediscovering familiar scents, before heading toward the street- side deck and the front door.

Ellie opened the door before I had a chance to knock.

"I was wondering if you'd be by," Ellie greeted me with a lack of enthusiasm.

"Kelly said you were sick. I was concerned and wanted to check on you."

"I'm fine," Ellie offered.

I looked at the dark circles under her eyes and the stringy hair that framed her face. She looked like she had been crying. A lot. Normally, Ellie took care with her appearance, but it looked like she'd slept in the sweatpants, T-shirt, and cardigan sweater she was wearing.

"It's a nice day. Do you want to sit out here on the deck and chat?" I asked.

I looked behind Ellie to see that the living area of the boathouse was a mess, which really worried me since Ellie was obsessively clean.

She looked like she might refuse my suggestion but then shrugged and stepped out onto the deck, closing the door behind her. She pulled her sweater around her shoulders as she took a seat in the sun. Charlie—sensing her distress, I imagine—curled up at her feet, placing one furry paw on the tip of her tennis shoe.

"Do you want to tell me what's going on?" I asked.

Ellie didn't say anything.

"Is it a guy?" I fished.

"No, it's not a guy."

"Lack of a guy?"

"No, it's not that either."

"Then what is it?" I asked. "Kelly said you went to the doctor. Are you sick?"

Ellie took a deep breath and looked directly at me. "I didn't go to a regular doctor. I went to a clinic to look into the process of obtaining a sperm donor."

"I thought you were going to wait."

"I did wait."

Ellie had a point. She'd only promised to wait ninety days, and it had been more than that since she'd first broached the subject.

"Yeah, you did. I'm sorry I interrupted. Go on."

"Part of the process of taking advantage of the services the clinic offers is having a physical to assess your overall health and the likelihood of a successful impregnation."

Uh-oh. I think I could see where this was going.

"I won't bore you with the details, but the end result was that my tests indicate that I have less than a ten-percent chance of becoming pregnant by any means. Ever."

"Oh, El." I got up from my chair, knelt down in front of her, and hugged her. "I'm so sorry."

"I cannot accept," she sobbed, "the fact that I may never have children of my own."

"I know." I hugged her tighter, my own tears streaming down my face.

"I've spent the past week trying to gain some perspective, but it's been so hard to let go of everything I've dreamed of."

I have many fine qualities, but I'm afraid one of them isn't the ability to find the right thing to say at critical times like this. Ellie is a born comforter. If our roles were reversed, she'd know exactly what to say to make things better, but I'm not Ellie, and I know that the likelihood of saying something that will make things worse is actually pretty high, so I kept quiet and hugged her as tight as I could as my best friend and I wept out her pain.

After her tears had subsided, I went into the house in search of a tissue. "Is there anything you can do?" I asked after I'd returned to the deck and she'd pulled herself together.

"There are treatments, all expensive, none covered by insurance. None are guaranteed and most provide only a slightly better chance at a successful pregnancy than I already have. I thought about looking into surgical options, which give me the best chance I'm likely to have, but given the fact that I'm unmarried, I don't present a high priority as far as most doctors are concerned. The few doctors I spoke to encouraged me to wait. They said that new treatments are being developed every day, and perhaps by the time I'm ready . . ."

"But you feel ready now."

"I did." Ellie looked at me. "But, like I mentioned, I've agonized over this since I first found out and I think I'm beginning to get a little perspective. I don't want to go through all of that alone. If and when I fall in love and get married, then maybe."

I hugged Ellie one final time and then sat back down next to her.

She bent over to scratch Charlie behind the ears. "I think I might be ready to consider a puppy, as you suggested earlier. A puppy isn't a baby, and I'm sure a puppy won't fix everything, but now that you and Charlie are living with Zak, I find that I do get lonely at times. It would be nice to have someone to come home to."

"Now would be a good time," I affirmed. "Things have slowed down at the Beach Hut and are likely to remain slow over the winter. Puppies need a lot of attention the first few months, so it's important that you're around to provide the guidance the little guy or gal will need."

"I don't suppose you know of a slightly older dog that wouldn't need as much attention? I'd like a young dog, but perhaps not a brand-new puppy."

"Let me look around. I promise I'll find you the perfect dog."

Ellie smiled. "Thanks. And Zoe, can we keep my medical issues just between us for the time being? I don't really want Levi to know. At least not yet."

"It'll be our secret," I promised.

"I need a well-behaved older puppy for Ellie," I said to Jeremy the moment I walked through the front door of the log structure that houses Zoe's Zoo.

"Ellie's getting a puppy?" Jeremy asked. He was holding two of the kittens that had been brought in the previous week.

"Ellie *needs* a puppy," I emphasized as I reached for one of the little fuzz balls Jeremy was cuddling. "She's decided to give up her quest for a baby, at least for the time being, and she needs a dog to keep her company."

"I think it's best that she decided to wait. How old a puppy are you thinking?" Jeremy asked as he placed the kitten he was holding back into its cage.

"Ideally, we're looking for a dog that's still young enough to be fun and playful but is also house-trained, socialized, and has gone through basic obedience training."

"Does size or breed matter?"

I paused to consider what type of dog Ellie would like. She'd never owned a dog before, but she seemed to enjoy the various canines who had passed through my life and had never shown much of a preference toward one breed over another.

"No, I don't think so," I answered. "Ellie likes to hike, so perhaps a medium or large breed would be best. Not too big, though. She's living in the boathouse, so I'm not sure that a Saint Bernard or mastiff would be the best choice. Maybe a dog the size of a lab or retriever."

"I know a guy who breeds and trains German shepherds for police work. He usually starts off with four or five pups a year but eliminates puppies as he assesses their natural abilities. By the end of the year, he's usually down to one. He places the dogs he eliminates in qualified homes. The dogs he rejects are better bred and trained than any you're likely to find anywhere else. I can contact him if you want."

"That would be perfect." I placed the kitten I was holding back into the cage next to his brother. "Let me know what you find out. I want to get just the right pup, but it would be wonderful to find something right away."

"I'll call Peter after we discuss Gimp."

Gimp was the name we'd given the mountain lion who had come in with a broken leg.

"What's up with him?" I asked as I walked down the hall to my office with Jeremy tagging along behind.

"He's restless. Very restless. He's making the other animals nervous. I thought maybe we should talk to Scott about a sedative."

Normally, I hate to sedate animals unless we have to, but Gimp was a wild animal who was very efficient about letting everyone know that he wasn't happy about being caged. He tended to spend most of the day pacing and roaring.

"How long do we have him?"

"Just a few weeks. Once the cast comes off, they'll return him to the spot where they found him. His leg is healing great, but I do worry about him reinjuring it if we can't keep him quiet."

"Okay, call Scott. Maybe he can give him something to take the edge off. Anything else?" I asked as I picked up a pile of mail.

"Trenton Field called. He said he was returning your call. He tried your cell, but I guess you didn't answer. I told him that you often turned it off when you were in a meeting but would get back to him today."

"Okay, thanks. I'll call him back."

"Any news about the dead ghost hunter?" Jeremy asked. "Everyone is talking about him."

I tossed the mail back on the desk. "Not really. To be honest, I haven't even spoken to Salinger about the investigation. I'm really curious about what might have happened, but I've been busy, and I know Zak would prefer that I stay out of it. He thinks I'm going to put myself in danger by snooping around."

"Zak has a point. You do seem to have a knack for putting yourself in danger. I just figured you called Trenton because he'd spent time with the ghost hunter before he died. Everyone is talking about that too."

I walked across the room and opened the window. It really was a nice day. "Yeah," I answered. "That was the reason I called Trenton in the first place. Ethan mentioned that the men dined together, and I was curious. I don't suppose it would hurt to talk to him. No danger in that."

"If you do happen across anything interesting, fill me in. Adam Davenport's death is the talk of the town and it's nice to have a leg up on the local gossip."

I laughed. "If I hear anything juicy, you'll be the second one to know."

"I appreciate that. Before I forget, a reporter form the newspaper in Bryton Lake called. She wants to do a feature on you for a column she writes called 'Women Power.'"

"She wants to do a feature on me?"

"One of her good friends adopted a puppy from us last month. The woman came in looking for one type of dog and left with a different breed entirely. She's thrilled. The reporter indicated that the column would focus on your matchmaking superpower. She even referred to you as the 'pet matchmaker of our generation.'"

I smiled. "Really? I think I like that: Zoe Donovan, Pet Matchmaker."

"So should I set it up?"

"Give me her number and I'll call her. Maybe we can work in some publicity for the Zoo. It would be great to have all our charges adopted into cozy homes before the holidays."

"I'll look up her number and text it to you." Jeremy turned to leave.

"Let me know what you find out after talking to your friend about a pup for Ellie," I reminded him.

"I'll call him right now."

"Thanks." I headed back over to my desk to call Trenton. Jeremy had a point about being a step ahead of the local gossip. Even though I wasn't investigating the death, I supposed it couldn't hurt to hear what he had to say.

"Trenton, it's Zoe. I'm sorry I missed your call," I began after he answered on his end.

"Are you interested in parapsychology?"

"Only as far as it pertains to the dead ghost hunter who was found in the Henderson house."

"Ah, I should have known. What would you like to know?" Trenton asked.

"First of all, do you believe in ghosts?"

"So did *he* believe in ghosts?" Zak asked later that evening, as I was filling him in on my conversation with Trenton.

"He said that while he was open to the possibility of altered states of consciousness, and has seen some amazing research in the area, he wasn't willing to go so far as to say that he absolutely believed in the actual presence of ghosts as we were referring to them. He did say that it seemed Professor Davenport might have been on to something with his research, although, again, he was unwilling to state that a poltergeist might have frightened the man enough to cause his tumble down the stairs."

"I want to hear the whole story, but I'm going to grab a beer. Would you like some wine?" Zak asked.

"Yeah, I guess I'll take half a glass."

We were sitting outside on the deck overlooking the lake next to a roaring fire that was keeping us toasty warm. It really had been a beautiful autumn this year, and Zak and I were committed to taking advantage of every last minute of the awesome weather. I leaned back in my chair and looked out at the moon shining on the lake. The orange glow from Zak's lights from the front of the house gave an eerie feel to the otherwise dark night. I'd convinced him that the firelight was all that was needed in the back on this particular evening. I tossed another log on the fire and watched as the sap that hid in the crevices of the freshly cut pine snapped and sparked as it was exposed and ignited. Luckily, the fire pit had been built on the edge of the seating area, where the deck met the sandy beach, which separated the lake from the forest.

"Okay, so Trenton talked to Davenport," Zak said, picking up the conversation where we'd left off as he handed me my wine.

"Trenton said Adam Davenport had been doing research on the Henderson house for quite some time. He'd gathered as much information as he could by pulling old newspaper articles, obtaining copies of police reports, and digging into everything he could find concerning the history of the house. After taking into consideration everything he'd uncovered, he decided there was enough evidence to justify a trip to Ashton Falls. It seems he'd been hanging out at the Henderson house for the past two weeks. No one realized he was there because few people, other than the occasional drifter or the high-school party crowd, dared to venture out to the property."

"How did Trenton know he was in the area?" Zak wondered.

"Davenport contacted Trenton and asked if he'd be willing to meet and provide some background information about the house. Trenton agreed since they had a similar background."

"Similar background?" Zak asked as he stirred the coals and tossed another log on the fire.

"Although Davenport ventured into the field of parapsychology later in his career, his undergraduate work was in psychology, as was Trenton's. According to Trenton, they'd actually attended some of the same seminars in their early academic careers."

I took a sip of my wine as I gathered my thoughts. Zak really did buy the best wines. Prior to my relationship with him, I'd usually purchased whatever was on sale at the grocery store, but Zak had wine sent to the house from vineyards all over the world.

"So the men met for lunch . . ." Zak prompted.

I set my wine on the table next to my chair and tucked my legs up under my body. The temperature had dropped and in spite of the fire, my feet were getting cold.

"Trenton indicated that while the men had taken differing paths after completing their undergraduate work, they had many viewpoints in common," I said. "He told me that he shared what he knew about the history of the house, including the mysterious deaths that had occurred over the years, and Davenport provided small tidbits of information that Trenton had never known."

"Such as?"

"Such as the fact that Hezekiah Henderson wasn't the only Henderson to die in that house. According to Trenton, Hezekiah's grandparents died unexpectedly when Hezekiah's father was a young man. His father, an only child, inherited the house, and after marrying a young girl from the area, he settled in to raise a family. By the time Hezekiah reached his twenty-fifth birthday, his parents and siblings had all died. According to Trenton, Davenport felt that each of the deaths he looked into could have a supernatural cause as well as a logical one."

"Like what?" Zak sat forward in his chair. He took one of my bare feet and placed it in his lap. He began to massage away the tension in my entire body by skillfully working his magic on my foot.

"He didn't really go into a lot of detail. To be honest, I was in a hurry and didn't ask him to elaborate. He did say that in the one hundred fifty-odd years the house has existed, Davenport is the fifth person who died from falling down those same stairs."

"Okay, that's a little weird. And I didn't realize the house was that old."

"Trenton said Davenport told him that the place was originally built as a cabin and had been expanded many times since."

Zak frowned. "I'm surprised more people don't know that story. It seems pretty sensational."

"Hezekiah Henderson was an old man when I was a child. If I remember correctly, he was in his late eighties when he died. I was nine, so Pappy would have been around fifty. If Hezekiah was, say, eighty-five when he died, that would make him a good thirty-five years older than Pappy. If Hezekiah's family was dead by the time he was twenty-five, Pappy wouldn't even have been born yet."

"The town hadn't been incorporated back then," Zak added. "Which means there wouldn't have been a lot of recordkeeping."

"Yeah, and the newspaper in Bryon Lake wouldn't even have been in existence."

"How did Davenport find all of this out?" Zak wondered.

"Death records and personal accounts from the diaries of some of the mill workers who lived in the area during the days when it was used as a logging camp, among other things."

"So although Hezekiah lived a long life, dozens of others have died of mysterious causes over the years," Zak concluded. "Wow. It sort of makes you believe in the haunted house theory."

"I know. Right?"

I switched feet so that Zak could work on the left side of my body. Zak really does give the best foot rubs. He knows all the pressure points to address to create total body relaxation.

"So Davenport comes to get a 'feel' for the house and ends up dead," Zak continued after I'd made the switch. "I agree that the whole thing is odd and sort of spooky, but I think it's best we don't get too caught up in the theory that a ghost or otherworldly spirit is guilty of scaring Davenport down the stairs."

"Why not?" I groaned as Zak found an extra-sensitive spot.

"Assuming the man didn't simply fall, he was most likely pushed, and there very well could be a real killer out there."

"That's basically what Trenton said," I admitted. "Although he did say that it seemed like there was more going on with Davenport than he communicated."

"Like what?" Zak asked.

"Trenton didn't really know. He said Davenport seemed extremely invested in the history of the house, and the personal detachment that most researchers try to bring to a project seemed to be skewed by something Davenport wasn't saying. Trenton didn't go so far as to say he was lying about his true purpose for investigating paranormal activity in the house, but he did say that his words seemed deliberate, and at times he became downright evasive."

"So Davenport thinks there may be more to the killings than meets the eye?" Zak began to work his way up my calf. I hadn't had a chance to go for a run in several days and my muscles felt tight, so Zak's magical hands felt *wonderful.*

"Not really," I answered. "Although he isn't completely convinced the killings were random either. He spoke to Salinger, who thinks the killer ghost theory is hogwash, so I assume he's focusing on locating a living, breathing killer. I feel like I should be doing something, but I'm not sure what that would be at this point."

"It's not your job to track down every killer who lands in the area," Zak reminded me.

"I know. Which is why I'm going to leave the investigation to Salinger for once. Besides, I'm going off the mountain tomorrow and will be gone most of the day."

Zak looked surprised. "Really? Where are you going?"

"To see a man about a dog."

# Chapter 6

## Wednesday, October 22

"I can't believe how excited I am." Ellie smiled as we drove through the valley toward the home of Peter Darwin, the breeder Jeremy had told me about the day before. Not only was he willing to meet Ellie to discuss placing a puppy with her but he happened to have a pup in need of placement. Talk about perfect timing.

"Remember, it's not a for-sure thing until he meets you," I warned her as we made the trip down the mountain. A rambling river paralleled the narrow, winding road as the thick evergreen forest gave way to the foothills, painted with autumn colors. "He wants to be certain that you and Shep are a good match before he agrees to the adoption."

"Yeah, I get it. You would do the same thing."

"Yes, I would."

Ellie took a deep breath and looked out the window. I could tell she was nervous, which, to be honest, sort of surprised me. When I'd first suggested a puppy, she hadn't been interested, and now she was acting like getting this puppy was the most important thing in her life.

"How old is Shep?" Ellie turned to face me.

"He's eight months old. Jeremy said he's smart and attentive and showed a lot of promise, but he suffered a broken leg when he was four months old and it didn't heal up well enough for him to be placed into police service. According to Jeremy, his limp isn't noticeable unless you know what you're looking for, and it doesn't hinder his ability to run or enjoy a normal life, but the screening process to become a law enforcement dog is tough. Shep is well trained and very friendly. Peter told Jeremy that he seems to prefer women and will make a good dog for a female handler."

"He sounds perfect." Ellie grinned.

I felt like it was the first genuine grin I'd seen from her in quite some time.

"I know I never really cared about having a dog," Ellie added, "but I'm really happy you talked me into it."

*I talked her into it?*

"If I'm approved, when can I bring him home?"

I slowed to maneuver an extra-tight S curve. "Today, as far as I know. We can stop at the animal supply store in Bryton Lake and pick up everything you'll need. We'll need to keep him on the same food the breeder has him on, at least for a while. If you decide to change the brand, you'll need to do so slowly."

"I'm sure that whatever food the breeder uses will be fine for me. I don't have a lot of experience feeding dogs, so I plan to follow the breeder's recommendations to a T."

"That's usually best."

"I know I've already said this like ten times, but I really hope this works out. I love living in your boathouse, but it's pretty isolated. I think I'll feel better with a big dog on the premises."

"Remember, it's not for sure."

"I know."

I was taking a chance bringing Ellie to meet Shep when she was so vulnerable. God, I hoped this worked out. I was afraid if it didn't, she'd spiral into a depression I wasn't entirely sure how to deal with. Ellie seemed to like dogs and was super good with Charlie and the other dogs in my life, but she'd never had one of her own. Her mom had never wanted animals in the house when Ellie was growing up, and when she got her own apartment, animals weren't allowed. I hoped she understood the time commitment that comes with having a canine buddy.

Of course, I reminded myself, although I'm pretty sure I didn't do or say anything to actually talk her into getting a dog, it had been my idea in the first place. I had a flexible schedule, so I'd simply make the commitment to help out as needed, and if this dog didn't work out for some reason, I'd find her an equally awesome replacement.

"We have another thirty minutes at least until we get to Peter's property; maybe we should use this time to talk about food for the Halloween party," I suggested.

"Okay, I'm game." Ellie shifted in her seat so she could reach her purse. She pulled out a small notepad and a pen. "What type are you thinking?"

"Zak has gone all-out with the decorations and is building coffins that he plans to fill with dry ice to serve the food. I was thinking we could do theme food, like mummy dogs."

Ellie clicked the end of the pen as she thought about the situation. "I have an idea to make wontons shaped like bats. I could do a couple of different fillings. Crab and cream cheese are my favorites. I also have a recipe for jalapeño popper wontons, as well as a sausage-based wonton that everyone seems to love."

"Sounds perfect. What else do you have?" I hoped our talk about food would help Ellie relax before we arrived at the ranch.

"Deviled eggs made up to look like eyeballs are easy and tasty, and I can make cheese balls shaped like jack-o'-lanterns or spiders in several different flavors. We can make up some roaches and other bugs using figs and other veggies and add them to any dips we want to provide, and we can make homemade pizzas with jack-o'-lantern faces on them."

"Levi will be looking for chicken wings."

Ellie shrugged. "I'm sure I can come up with a spooky way to present them. Give me a day or two to really think about it and I'm sure we can come up with a variety of offerings. Did you ever decide on a costume?"

"Zak is going to go as Frankenstein and I'm going to be the Bride of Frankenstein."

"Speaking of brides, did you ever have the talk?" Ellie asked.

"No, not in so many words. I guess we decided to put the subject of marriage on the back burner for now. I know he loves me and wants to marry me, and I want to marry him too. Someday," I qualified. "I imagine it will come up again at some point, and I'm hoping I'll be ready to say yes with the enthusiasm and certainty he deserves. How about you? Have you come up with a costume?"

I made a left-hand turn off the highway to a narrow county road lined with aspens in full autumn color. The unirrigated pastures had turned brown, providing a striking contrast to the yellows and oranges.

"I still can't decide." Ellie sighed. "Please don't take this wrong, but I'm not all that excited about the party this year. Not that it won't be awesome. It's just that you're going with Zak and Levi is going with Darla, which leaves me to play the third wheel—or I guess I should say fifth wheel."

"You could come with Kelly," I offered.

"Kelly is bringing a date. *Everyone* is coming with a date."

I felt bad for Ellie. I realized she might not be all that far off with her assertion that everyone was coming with a date. I knew Jeremy was going to attend with Jessica, and my other assistant, Tiffany, was coming with our veterinarian, Scott. As I thought about the situation, I realized Ellie could very well be the only person who wasn't paired up. Suddenly, I had a new mission to add to the fifty others I was already juggling: find Ellie a date, and not just any date, an awesome date.

"Oh, hey." Ellie interrupted my thoughts. "It looks like we're here."

I pulled onto a dirt road that served as a private drive. The ranch was far enough off the beaten path so as to appear to be totally isolated. There was a large sign that read DARWIN HORSE RANCH AND K-9 ACADEMY. The large ranch-style house was surrounded by miles upon miles of green pasture that apparently was irrigated and divided into neat sections with white fences. Each pasture was dotted with happy residents grazing in the warm afternoon sun.

"Wow, it's really beautiful," Ellie gushed.

"Yeah, it's awesome. Peter said to meet him in at the kennel, which must be that white building to the left."

"Yeah, the red building is definitely a barn, and the white one looks like it has individual dog runs attached," Ellie said.

I slowed my truck to a crawl to avoid kicking up more dust than I had to on the dirt road. As I pulled up in front of the white building, a tall man who I would guess was in his midthirties walked out to greet us. He was dressed in faded jeans and a light blue T-shirt. He wore a baseball cap with the San Francisco GIANTS logo on his head.

"Zoe?" he greeted me.

I hopped down out of my monster of a truck.

"Yes, I'm Jeremy's friend, Zoe Donovan, and this is my friend, Ellie Davis." I reached out to shake the man's hand. "Your ranch is gorgeous."

"Thank you; I like it. The land has been in my family for four generations and I'm quite proud of it."

"I didn't realize you raised horses as well as dogs," I commented as a herd of horses trotted by in a nearby pasture.

"My father and his father before him were horse breeders, but I've always had a fondness for dogs and dog training, so when I inherited the ranch, I added the dogs."

"Do you train the horses as well?" I asked.

Peter nodded toward a man sitting on the fence of one of the corrals, watching another man dressed in Levi's and a plaid shirt put a large black horse through a series of commands. "Actually, I turned the horses over to my dad's best friend, Chip, who has lived on the ranch since before I was born. I enjoy the horses, but I really prefer to work with dogs. Chip has a way with horses that only comes from decades of working with them."

"So you train the dogs for law enforcement?" I asked.

"I do train dogs for law-enforcement agencies, but I raise and train guide and service dogs as well. I have two full-time assistants, but I still keep darn right busy."

"I can imagine."

"Can we meet Shep?" Ellie entered the conversation.

"How about we chat a bit first?" Peter suggested. "There's a table and some chairs inside, if you'd like to follow me."

"Okay." Ellie trailed along behind the man, who was quite the looker, as we made our way to the office that was located in the front of the white building we had parked near.

"Please take a seat," Peter directed Ellie.

"What would you like to know?" she asked, fidgeting as she sat down and waited for him to begin.

"Have you had a dog before?" Peter asked.

Ellie hesitated. "No. Is that a problem?"

Peter shrugged. "Not necessarily. Are you familiar with the handling and care of dogs?"

"I pet sit for Zoe all the time."

"And she's a fantastic pet sitter," I added as I walked around the large room, looking at the photos on the wall. "My dog Charlie absolutely adores her."

"Tell me a bit about your home situation."

"Home situation?"

"Are you married? Single? Do you have children? Other pets? Do you rent or own your home? House or apartment? That sort of thing."

"Oh, okay."

Ellie seemed nervous, but I thought she was doing fine, so I decided to wander around the office while they chatted. The walls were covered with photos of men with horses. Some of the photos were in black and white, while others looked to have been taken fairly recently. The photos were interesting; not only could you see the progression of men who had lived and worked on the ranch but the ranch infrastructure as well. The earliest photos showed a house a third of the size of the current structure, with only a single red barn. As we'd driven up, I'd noticed at least four large buildings, which I guessed housed either dogs or horses.

There were also photos of men and women I assumed were family members, as well as some from the key moments of Peter's life. In one photo he stood proudly in a cap and gown alongside a group of friends, and others were of the various proms he'd attended, as well as several of him alongside various dogs.

"I'm sorry to interrupt," I said as I did just that, "but this man standing with the group in front of the lake: who is he?"

Peter looked up from the paperwork he was filling out as he spoke to Ellie. "His name is Adam Davenport. The photo was taken the summer after I graduated high school. My friend Puk talked me into getting a job with him at the summer camp they used to have at Star Lake."

"Adam was a counselor?"

"Yeah, everyone in the photo was. I only worked at Star Lake that one year, but Puk went back every summer until they closed the camp down after those counselors died."

Star Lake is only about five miles from Ashton Falls. The privately owned lake had been home to a summer camp for inner-city kids until it closed thirteen years ago. I was only a kid at the time of the incident, but I vaguely remembered that although it was strictly against camp rules to leave the area or to possess alcoholic beverages, a group of counselors snuck away to the Henderson house to party one summer night. Three people had died and another was missing before the night was over.

"Was Puk one of the counselors who snuck off?" I wondered.

"No; he was working out at the camp when the tragedy occurred," Peter informed me.

I looked back at the photo. There were eighteen men and women posed in front of the lake. There was one woman who looked sort of familiar, although I couldn't place her. I didn't recognize any of the others, so my guess was that none of the counselors who were on staff with Peter that year had remained in the area. I had no way of knowing how many of the counselors in the photo were still on staff by the time the accident occurred. For all I knew, with the exception of Puk, the staff could have turned over completely. It did, however, make sense that at least a few had remained. I tried to decide if the man in the back left-hand corner was a younger version of the man I'd seen in the costume shop that night.

"Was Adam Davenport working at the camp that year as well?"

"Yes, I believe he was. Why do you ask?"

"Mr. Davenport recently came to Ashton Falls to do research on the Henderson house. I'm afraid he's dead."

"Dead? What happened?"

I explained to Peter Darwin the series of events leading up to and preceding Mr. Davenport's death, while he filled me in on what he knew about the incident thirteen years ago. I felt bad that Ellie's bid to adopt a new puppy was being waylaid by our conversation, but eventually Ellie did meet Shep, it was love at first sight on both sides, and soon Ellie and I were packing up the truck to head back up the mountain.

"Thank you so much." Ellie hugged Peter for what seemed like the hundredth time. "I'll take such good care of Shep; I promise. And feel free to come by to check on him any time you're in the area."

"I just might do that." Peter smiled as he helped to load Shep into the back of my truck, which had been specially outfitted to transport both large and small animals. "I like to keep track of my kids."

"Do you have a lot of dogs to keep track of?" Ellie wondered as she petted Shep one last time before closing the door of the crate that would ensure a safe trip home.

"Hundreds. But each and every one is dear to me."

"Well, please do come and visit Shep. We'd both enjoy spending time with you at the lake. It's beautiful in the valley, but nothing compares with October at the lake."

Was Ellie actually flirting with Peter Darwin? It seemed like it, and if I read things correctly, Peter didn't mind the attention at all.

"I planned to make the trip up the mountain to attend the Haunted Hamlet this weekend. Perhaps we can meet up somewhere?" Peter suggested.

"I'm working the zombie run in the morning on Saturday, but maybe Friday evening or Saturday afternoon? We have a new event this year. It's a haunted hayride, which promises fun for all who dare to venture into the ghostly forest."

"Perhaps Friday." Peter smiled. "I have your number; I'll call you to confirm a time and place."

*Wow, way to go, Ellie.* She'd come away from this trip with both a dog and a date, while all I'd managed to acquire was a clue to a murder mystery I'd sworn to myself I'd stay out of.

"Do you mind if we stop by the hardware store so I can try to talk to Puk?" I asked Ellie as we drove back down the dirt road connecting Peter's ranch to the county road that led to the highway.

Peter had shared that Puk, whose real name was John Pukman, owned Bryton Lake Hardware and could usually be found there at this time of day. If he remembered anything about the night the campers were killed, I wanted to have the chance to interview him before Salinger realized he could be a good lead in the murder investigation. Not that Salinger and I weren't getting along much better than we had originally; it was just that I still didn't put a lot of faith in the man's detective skills. He was okay at maintaining order in our community when it came to the easy stuff, like petty theft and handing out speeding tickets, but when it came to murder . . .

"Not at all," Ellie said. "Shep and I will take a walk around that park just down the street. It'll give us a chance to get to know each other. He really is a great dog."

"Yeah, he's a sweetie. I didn't realize he'd be a long-haired shepherd. He's going to require extra brushing, but his coat is gorgeous."

"Remind me to pick up a good brush and the other supplies I might need when we're at the feed store. I hope they're still open."

"They stay open late on weeknights," I confirmed.

"So do you think this Puk knows anything that can help explain Adam Davenport's death?" Ellie wondered.

"I don't know. Maybe. It just seems to be a huge coincidence that he comes to Ashton Falls to do research on a house where a terrible tragedy occurred at which he may have been present, and then turns up dead in that very same house thirteen years later."

"It does seem sort of spooky. I know the whole town was in an uproar when those counselors died, but other than the fact that the deaths were classified as 'mysterious,' I don't remember a whole lot about them."

"Three counselors died while at the Henderson house. According to Trenton, one of the girls fell down the stairs, another was hit on the head, and one of the boys ran out of the house and was hit by a car that was fleeing the scene. A fourth counselor, another guy, disappeared and was never heard from again. Most people believe the missing counselor killed the others and then fled, but no one has ever figured out why."

By the time Ellie, Shep, and I got back to Ashton Falls it was time for me to leave for book club. Normally, it's on Thursdays, but with the opening of Haunted Hamlet the next night, we'd decided to move it up a day. Apparently, Wednesday really wasn't the best day for many of our members; as of the official start time, only Pappy, Hazel, Nick, and I had arrived.

"We can give it a few more minutes, but then I say we vote to table the discussion until next week," Hazel suggested.

That was fine with me. After the day I'd had, I was exhausted and anxious to get home to Zak and Charlie. Not that sitting in front of the warm fire Hazel had built in her brick fireplace wasn't pleasant. In fact, with the addition of the delicious wine she'd provided, I found that it was close to impossible not to nod off.

"Are you planning to come to the library for the Halloween party tomorrow?" Hazel asked me. "Your mom will be reading to the preschoolers from our selection of seasonal favorites."

"I'd like to come if I can work it out. What time is it?"

"We'll start at ten and be done by noon. We spent the day decorating the children's room, and a couple of our volunteers are bringing cupcakes."

"Can I bring Charlie?"

"Certainly, if you'd like."

Charlie was spending more time at home now that I lived with Zak and Bella, but I still tried to bring him into town with me as often as was convenient. Charlie enjoyed hanging out with the dog Zak had adopted in July, when her human was forced to move to a retirement community, but he loved kids, and I knew he'd be thrilled to attend the party at the library.

"So how did everything work out with Ellie and the pup?" Pappy joined the conversation. I'd mentioned to him the previous evening that we were making the trip down the mountain to look into adopting a German shepherd.

"It went really well. We haven't introduced him to Charlie and Bella yet, but I'm sure they'll all get along great, as long as poor Charlie doesn't get trampled on."

While Charlie weighs less than forty pounds, Shep probably weighs close to a hundred, and Bella, a golden retriever/Newfoundland mix, weighs close to one-fifty.

"Your dad has big dogs and Charlie does fine," Pappy told me.

"That's true, but Shep is a puppy, and a bit more energetic than Dad's dogs."

My dad and mom have three dogs between them. Tucker, a golden retriever, had been with Dad since he was a pup. He's getting on in years and tends to enjoy sleeping the day away about as much as anything. Last October, I talked Dad into adopting a yellow lab whose owner also had to move to an assisted living facility. Kiva has a bit more energy than Tucker but likewise is happy to lounge for much of the day. The third dog in the family, Sophie, is a rescue my mom fell in love with while pet sitting for me during the time I brought the pregnant terrier to the boathouse to have her pups.

"I'm glad the adoption worked out. Poor Ellie has had a rough time as of late," Hazel added.

"Yeah, it's been a tough few months. She did manage not only to get a puppy but a date out of the excursion to Peter Darwin's ranch, though."

I filled the others in on the chemistry I sensed between Ellie and Peter, and the date they'd set up.

"Good for her," Nick said, joining the conversation. "Peter Darwin is a good guy."

"You know him?" I asked.

"We have some friends in common, so we've played golf a few times."

"Did you know he was a counselor at Star Lake when the camp was open?" I asked.

"No, I don't know that he's ever mentioned it."

"He has a photo of a group of counselors in his office. You know who else was a counselor at the same time? Adam Davenport," I supplied without waiting for an answer.

"Our parapsychologist?" Pappy asked.

"One and the same. Peter told me he only worked at the camp for one summer, but Adam came back every summer until it closed down. I spoke to a man who goes by the name of Puk today. He's another friend of Peter's. He was hired on at the camp the same year Peter was, but he stayed with the program until they shut down. He had some interesting things to say about what went on the night those kids died."

Nick moved forward so that he was barely still on the chair he was sitting on. "Do tell. What did he say?"

I took a sip of my wine and settled in for the interesting tale. It was nice to have all eyes in the room on me as Nick, Pappy, and Hazel waited for me to continue.

"According to Puk, Davenport told him that strange things happened at the Henderson house that night. Davenport was there, one of the few who survived. It seems the survivors all swore never to tell anyone what actually happened at the party, so Puk didn't have a lot of details. He did say that he knew the name of one other counselor who was in the house that night."

"Someone we might know?" Pappy asked.

"His name is Griff Longiness. He moved away after the incident but came back to Ashton Falls last year."

"Odd that he'd move back to the very place where something so terrifying occurred," Pappy pointed out.

"Yeah, I thought the same thing, which makes him suspect number one in Davenport's death, as far as I'm concerned."

# Chapter 7

## Thursday, October 23

After spending the morning at the Zoo, digging through the mountain of paperwork on my desk, I called Zak and asked if he and Bella would like to join Charlie and me for lunch in the park. It was another in a string of gorgeous autumn days and it seemed a waste to remain indoors for even one more minute. Jeremy and Tiffany seemed to have things handled at the Zoo, so it was the perfect time to spend the afternoon with my man.

"I'm glad you suggested this," Zak said as he unpacked the sandwiches and soup he'd picked up from Ellie's. "You've been so busy that I've barely seen you."

"I know." I slid onto one of the picnic benches in the sun. "I need to try to focus my energy a little better. I totally missed the Halloween party at the library, which I told Hazel I'd try to attend."

"You have a lot going on right now," Zak sympathized. "Is everything set for the opening of Haunted Hamlet tonight?"

"Almost. I need to buy some candy for the kiddie carnival. I thought I'd stop at the market after we finish here."

"Bella and I will come with you," Zak offered. "What kind of candy are you thinking?"

I shrugged. "I need several thousand pieces since we're giving it out to the children who don't win bigger prizes. I was thinking maybe bubble gum or suckers; the type of thing that comes a hundred to a bag and only costs a few bucks."

Zak frowned. "You can't give a kid a single stick of gum as a prize. Let's get candy bars. Full-size Milky Ways, Snickers, and Twix. I'll donate them."

"Buying several thousand full-size candy bars will cost a fortune."

Zak smiled. "I just happen to have one."

"Okay." I shrugged. "But as long as we're buying candy bars, we need to get Baby Ruths and Butterfingers. They're my favorites. And the local market may not have the inventory we need. You may need to run down to the grocery warehouse in Bryton Lake."

"Let's check with Ernie first. If he has what we need, I'd rather buy locally. Is there anything else we need for the carnival as long as we're going to the store?"

Charlie looked at Zak and barked.

"I think Charlie wants to remind us that we're out of dog biscuits." I laughed.

"Don't worry." Zak scratched his head. "I won't forget the dog treats."

"Maybe we should have a selection of treats for any dogs that show up at the carnival with their humans," I said. Normally, I wouldn't go to the expense for such a well-attended event, but as long as we were spending Zak's money . . .

"Speaking of treats, I volunteered to work at the snack bar tomorrow afternoon," Zak informed me.

"Ellie wants us to join her and Peter for the haunted hayride. What time will you be done?"

"No later than five. I should be done in plenty of time to meet you guys. Is Levi joining us?"

"Probably. I invited him. I just hope it isn't weird for everyone to get together so early in Ellie's new relationship."

"You think there *is* a relationship?" Zak asked.

"I don't know for sure, but there was definite sparkage, so maybe. This soup is really good. It sort of tastes like a loaded baked potato."

"Ellie gave me a taste when I picked up the sandwiches. I thought you'd like it, so I asked her to add some to my order. She threw in a couple of pumpkin cookies as well."

"I'm glad we decided to do this." I smiled. "It's nice to take a short breather before I tackle the rest of the day."

"Is there anything else I can help you with other than the candy?" Zak asked.

"I made an appointment to talk to Griff Longiness at three. It would be great if you could come along for the interview."

"I thought you were going to stay away from the investigation into Adam Davenport's death."

"I am. It's just that the more I find out about the events that occurred at the Henderson house, the more curious I become. A group of counselors go to a deserted house to party, three turn up dead and one goes missing, and the cops are never able to piece together who was in attendance and what happened that night. It sounds like the plot for a horror movie."

"So you aren't investigating Adam Davenport's death, but you *are* investigating the deaths of the counselors thirteen years ago."

"Exactly. Will you help?"

Zak shrugged. "Sure; why not?"

"Maybe we should drop the dogs off at home before we head to the store," I said. "We can buy the candy, deliver it to the community center, and go to talk to Griff."

"Sounds like a date," Zak agreed.

"So what did you think?" I asked Zak as we strolled hand in hand through the pumpkin patch after meeting with Griff Longiness. I had volunteered to carve some pumpkins for the pumpkin walk that weekend and I'd never gotten around to buying any. Since I had Zak to help me, it seemed like the perfect opportunity.

"I think Griff is a man with a secret," Zak said as we searched the colorful hillside for perfect gourds.

"Yeah, I got the same feeling. On the surface, he seemed to be willing to discuss what occurred that night, but there were a lot of holes in his story." I picked up a pumpkin and turned it in my hands to check for roundness.

"It was almost as if he fed us exactly what he wanted us to know," Zak speculated. "His answers to our questions seemed almost rehearsed."

"In retrospect, maybe we should have just popped in on him rather than giving him time to plan a strategy. Still, I think the interview was worthwhile."

One of the more useful pieces of information Griff had shared was the identity of the other people present at the Henderson house that night. There were eight counselors in addition to Griff Longiness: Adam Davenport, who died in the house a few days ago; George Hingleman, who was hit by a car and died the night of the party; Drake Bollington, who moved from the area and, as far as Griff knew, had never returned; Carol Overall, who died after being hit in the head by a flying object; Rachael Jolie, who died after falling down the stairs; Dawn Highlander, who still lived in the area; Marie Good, who had since moved; and Bart Coleman, who'd disappeared that night and had never been seen again. The deputy who investigated the deaths believed that Bart killed George, Carol, and Rachael, and then took off, but Griff seemed to indicate there was more to the story than anyone really knew, although he was unwilling to go into much detail.

"I was thinking, now that we have the names of the survivors, we should try to interview the others." I set the pumpkin I'd been holding in the wagon Zak pulled behind him to carry the ones we selected.

"Of the original nine counselors at the Henderson house that night, five are still alive. We already talked to Griff, so that leaves Drake Bollinger, Marie Good, Dawn Highlander, and Bart Coleman. No one knows where Bart is or if he's even still alive, so we should start with one of the other three."

"We know Dawn is still in the area. I guess we can start with her," Zak suggested.

"Should we go now?" I asked.

Zak shrugged. "Might as well. I'll pay for these and you can grab us some cider for the road."

Ordinarily, I'd be less than certain that we could get a witness to discuss such a horrific night, but

Dawn had a crush on Zak, who tended to come into the diner on a regular basis, so I was certain if he asked nicely she'd willingly do whatever he requested. The minute we revealed the purpose of his invitation to share a cup of coffee with us, Dawn's face turned from sunny and slightly flushed to clouded and cautious.

"I'm not sure I can tell you anything you don't already know," she offered hesitantly.

Zak smiled at her. "We understand that the event was very traumatic for you, and it's been a very long time. We hoped that you could simply verify some things we've already learned from other sources."

Dawn relaxed a bit. "Oh, okay. I guess that would be fine."

"Why don't you just start by telling us what you remember?" Zak suggested.

Dawn fidgeted around in the booth a bit before settling in to tell us her story. "One of the other counselors, Rachael Jolie, told me that one of the guys she'd hung out with that afternoon had scored some pot and a group of them were going to some old abandoned house to smoke it. She asked me if I wanted to come along." Dawn looked down at her hands, which were folded in her lap. "I was a big partier back then, so I went. I've regretted that decision every day of my life."

"We've all done things we regret," I shared in an attempt to lighten the mood. Dawn seemed nervous about admitting her role in the affair, and I guess I didn't blame her. "I think sometimes it's our mistakes that make us better people in the long run."

Dawn looked up. She seemed relieved that we weren't there to judge her.

"Okay, so you went to the house with Rachael," Zak said to get her to continue.

Dawn looked at Zak. "When Rachael and I arrived at the house, there were seven other counselors, plus the girlfriend of one of the guys."

"Girlfriend?" I asked. "Do you remember her name?"

"No. We didn't speak to each other that night and we haven't spoken since, although I think she might have been from Bryton Lake."

Griff hadn't mentioned a girlfriend or anyone else other than the nine counselors.

"Do you know who she was with?" I asked.

"No, I'm sorry. I don't really remember. The whole night is sort of a blur."

Dawn sat back in the booth and looked out the window. She seemed to be lost in thought, which I suppose I understood, given the questions we were asking.

"You're doing great," Zak said. "What happened next?"

"It was cold out, so one of the others suggested that we head upstairs to the second floor, where there was a decent-looking fireplace already filled with wood."

"The fire was already built?" I asked.

"Yeah, there was wood and paper already in the fireplace, and extra wood nearby."

*Interesting.*

"Go on," I encouraged.

"Some of the counselors had brought alcohol, so after we lit the fire we all started smoking and drinking. Looking back on it, I think there was something in the pot because everyone started acting really weird."

"Weird how?" Zak asked.

Dawn shrugged. "Just different than people usually act when they smoke pot. Instead of everyone getting silly and mellow, it seemed like the group took on a sort of manic mood. It got worse when strange stuff started happening."

"What sort of strange stuff?" Zak asked.

Dawn looked uncertain. "I'm not sure if I should say. We all promised not to."

"Griff already told us quite a lot. We just wanted to get another perspective," I pushed.

Dawn looked at Zak, who smiled at her reassuringly.

"It started with all sorts of strange sounds coming from the attic."

"What sort of sounds?" Zak asked.

"There was a lot of thumping and there was this humming sound I can't really describe. Everyone commented on it, and looking back, I know we should have been scared, but we weren't. Everyone started telling jokes about partying with ghosts, and our overall mood was pretty darn close to euphoria."

"So when did the really weird stuff start happening?" Zak asked.

Dawn fidgeted with a napkin while she gathered her thoughts. I felt bad that we were asking her to relive such a horrible memory, but I had the feeling that the deaths of the counselors thirteen years ago and the death of Adam Davenport now were somehow related.

"I guess the first really strange thing that happened was this lamp that flew across the room and hit Carol in the head. She was out cold, but she was breathing, and she wasn't really bleeding all that much, so we moved her to the side of the room and kept partying. I can see now how dumb that was, but like I said, whatever was in that pot made everyone really happy. I had no idea that Carol was really hurt and I don't think anyone else did either."

"So what happened after Carol was hit in the head?" I asked.

"Nothing at first, and then the fire went all wonky. Flames were shooting out and there were embers flying everywhere. I'm pretty sure whoever built the fire put firecrackers in some sort of fire-resistant container that took a while to burn through. One of the burning embers got caught in Rachael's hair and she took off running."

I could see that the memory was difficult for Dawn. A tear slid down her cheek.

"She tripped on something and fell down the stairs. Unlike Carol, who we thought was fine, we knew right off that Rachael was dead."

Dawn wiped the tear from her face with the back of her hand.

"After that, everyone freaked out. People started yelling and running toward the cars. I'd come with Rachael, so I wasn't sure what to do, but Griff grabbed my arm and pulled me into his car. This guy George ran right in front of us. Griff hit him and . . ."

Dawn closed her eyes and dropped her head.

"It's okay." Zak took her hand in his.

"It wasn't Griff's fault," Dawn insisted. "There was no way he could have stopped in time. It seemed like that kid couldn't even see us. He was running around and screaming, paying no attention to where he was going." She looked at Zak for a moment. "I probably shouldn't have told you who was driving. We all promised not to."

"It's okay. What happened occurred a long time ago."

"So at this point, when everyone was driving away, can you remember where the others were?" I brought the conversation back around to the subject at hand.

Dawn paused to think about it. "Rachael was still lying at the foot of the stairs, I was with Griff in his car, George was lying on the ground near our car, and Marie took off with Adam in Adam's car." Dawn bit her lip as she tried to remember. "I don't know where Drake was. He might have already left. I do remember that Bart went back in to get Carol, who we thought was still alive."

"Bart is the counselor who turned up missing?" I confirmed.

"Yeah. No one ever did find out what happened to him."

"Were you aware at the time that Bart never came back out of the house?"

She shook her head. "Griff pulled George's body to the side of the drive and we left. He was pretty freaked out. He was worried about getting in trouble for what happened, so he made me promise not to tell."

"Who else knew that Griff hit George?"

Dawn thought about it. "Bart saw what happened. Marie and Adam had already left, and like I said, we were pretty sure Drake had left as well."

"And the girl whose name you don't remember?" I asked. "Do you remember where she was?"

Dawn frowned. "No. I'm sorry. I think she'd already left. I'm really not sure. It was all so crazy."

"And after that night?" I wondered.

"No one other than those of us at the party knew that anything had happened until the next day. Those of us who were able to snuck back into our cabins and acted like we'd never even left."

"Then what happened?" Zak asked.

"When the four missing counselors didn't show up at breakfast, the administration called the cops. Eventually, they found the three bodies. No one ever did find out what happened to Bart. Maybe he just got scared and took off. The sheriff asked everyone at the camp a bunch of questions, but we'd all agreed not to say anything about what happened at the house. We kept saying that we didn't know anything and after a while they stopped asking."

"And in all of these years you've never told anyone what really happened?" Zak asked.

"Not until now."

# Chapter 8

## Friday, October 24

When Charlie and I got to the Zoo the next morning, Jeremy informed me that he might have tracked down our mama cat's owner. Apparently, someone had reported a missing cat matching her description a couple of weeks earlier. Taking in strays can be a risky venture when it comes to your heart. While I hadn't had time to bond with the mother cat and her offspring, and hoped that we would find her owner if she had one, I couldn't help but be reminded of the heartache I'd suffered when I'd taken in a pregnant dog named Maggie the previous fall. Maggie was a rescue dog from a puppy mill, and it never occurred to me that she had owners who were looking for and missed her. I gave Maggie my heart only to have it ripped apart when the little girl who loved her was located and I had to let Maggie go.

Of course, I have warm memories of Maggie as well. Zak and I helped deliver her pups, and I can remember sitting by her side for hours, watching her nurse the little darlings. And it did feel good to reunite the little girl with the dog she loved. Reuniting animals with their owners is part of why I went into the animal rescue and rehabilitation profession in the first place.

After meeting with the woman and confirming that the cat we found was indeed hers, I called Zak and arranged for her to pick the mom and kittens up at the house. I'd had a long discussion with her about finding perfect homes for the babies and having the mama spayed once the kittens were weaned. Luckily, she agreed to both.

While he had me on the line, Zak informed me that he'd come up with a phone number for Marie Good, who seemed disinclined to discuss the events of the evening in question. Zak filled me in on the small amount of information he did manage to get out of her, which I in turn shared with Jeremy, who had been listening in on bits of our conversation, after Zak and I hung up.

"Zak told her about Davenport?" Jeremy asked.

"He did. She told Zak that she was sorry to hear that he was dead, and that she really liked him. She indicated that of the counselors who attended the party that night, he seemed to be the most serious and down-to-earth."

"The whole thing was such a tragedy," Jeremy commented.

"It really was. She indicated that the things that happened that night had seemed supernatural in nature and couldn't be explained by logic or rational means," I informed my assistant.

"So she believes in ghosts?"

"Zak thinks what she believes is a lot worse than a ghost. He said she seemed really scared and even went as far as to say that the house was alive and out for revenge. Zak said she very sweetly asked him to keep her out of the current investigation. It seemed that, although she had moved across the country, she was still concerned for her own safety and wanted nothing to do with the house or its victims."

"Wow, spooky."

After I finished my chores at the Zoo, Charlie and I headed into town to help out with the Haunted Hamlet. The majority of the events would take place over the weekend, but the maze and hayride both opened today, as did the jack-o'-lantern viewing in the park. The pumpkin-carving contest would be held tomorrow, but for tonight, the gazebo would be used as the judging area for the annual bake-off. The bake-off was only open to amateurs, so Ellie wasn't eligible to participate; as she did most years, she'd agreed to serve as one of the judges.

"So how are the entries this year?" I asked Ellie, who was making her way from table to table, tasting the final products.

"Really delicious. As you know, the committee decided to have several rounds this year. Pies were first, followed by cakes, and now we're tasting cookies and cookie bars. By the time I get around to sweetbreads and muffins, I'm going to need elastic in my pants."

Ellie took a small bite of Mrs. Wailington's peanut butter cookie before complimenting her on the flavor and making a note on the judge's sheet attached to her clipboard.

"Many of the entries are very commonplace," Ellie whispered after stepping off to the side, where no one would be able to overhear her. "It seems if they made the requirements a bit more difficult, we wouldn't have as many entries. We had over twenty cookies entered in that one category alone."

I waved at Ellie's mom, Rosie, who was tasting a cookie at another table. "It's fun for average cooks to be able to enter. Not everyone can be culinarily gifted, like you and your mom."

"Yeah, I guess, but as a judge who has to taste every one, it feels like there are just too many chocolate chip cookies to really do justice to any one entry."

"What's been your favorite so far?" I asked as Ellie took a sip from her water bottle.

"Do you mean of the cookies I've tasted so far, or overall?"

"Overall."

Ellie thought about it. "I'm partial to pies, so my favorite overall would be the banana cream pie Mrs. Barker made. Although her daughter-in-law's blackberry pie was equally delicious. Oh, and then there was the ice cream pie with freshly churned apricot ice cream. Darn; now I'm getting hungry."

"You're welcome." I smiled. "I know cookies aren't your favorite, so I figured if I got you thinking about pies, you'd be able to finish the cookies."

"Clever."

"How many do you have left?" I wondered as Ellie headed back toward the judging area.

"Three more cookies and then seven sweetbreads and five muffins in about an hour."

"Too bad you couldn't enter your triple berry muffins or pumpkin spice bread. Either one is blue-ribbon worthy."

"I have a new muffin recipe I'm working on that's even better than the triple berry. I'll bring a few over when I get a chance."

My mouth was already beginning to water. Ellie was a genius at everything she made, but her muffins were the best I had ever tasted. She always seemed to get them light and fluffy, yet they held together when you ate them. I hated it when muffins crumbled in your hand when you took a bite or were so heavy you needed antacids to digest them.

"Where's Shep while you're eating your way into a larger pant size?" I asked.

Ellie greeted the woman at table eight before taking a bite of her German chocolate cookie bar. The obvious surprise on Ellie's face indicated that she liked it more than she'd thought she would. She praised the woman and then moved on to the next table before answering my question.

"Levi has Shep for the afternoon. He took him for a run and then to the beach. He's stopped by several times since I brought Shep home. They seem to really like each other. I wouldn't be surprised if Levi isn't the next friend to ask you to find the perfect dog."

"Levi doesn't like to be tied down," I pointed out.

Ellie frowned and dropped her eyes. Perhaps that wasn't the best thing to bring up.

"However," I added, "I bet that once he spends time with Shep, he'll find he'd like a little buddy of his very own."

"Maybe." Ellie shrugged, as if she didn't care, but I knew that she did.

"So is Peter still joining us tonight for the hayride?" I asked in an attempt to segue into a less sensitive subject.

Ellie smiled. "He is. I can't wait to show him around the Haunted Hamlet. I know he's been here before, but somehow this year seems special."

I noticed Willa waving to me from across the street. She probably had chores for me to do before I went off-duty for the day. "It looks like Willa needs me. Catch ya later?"

"We can meet at the hayride as planned, unless Willa talks you into filling one of the ghostly graveyard roles."

"She needs more people?"

"That's the rumor. If I were you, I'd be prepared with a really good excuse."

"The line for the haunted hayride goes all the way to the fence," Ellie observed later that evening. "I really thought we'd have fewer guests with the change in venue, but I guess people are excited to get a peek at something new. I hope Peter can find us okay."

"He'll find us," I assured my friend, who was looking nervously toward the festively decorated street. Luckily, Willa hadn't asked me to play a role in the event but rather to help Joel set up a few additional props he had decided on. If the spooky display I witnessed was any indication, the hayride was going to be a huge success.

"What time is Zak supposed to be here?" Ellie asked.

I looked at my watch. "He has another half hour at the snack bar, but I doubt we'll be at the front of the line by then. Oh look, there's my mom and dad."

I waved at them as they came toward us, my baby sister in her stroller. It had been two months since they'd finally tied the knot, and based on all appearances, they couldn't be happier.

"You dressed her up as a bunny rabbit," I gushed as I picked up Harper. She looked adorable in her fuzzy outfit and droopy ears.

"I figured it would be warm," Mom commented. "And she was born at Easter, so I figured it was appropriate that a bunny be her first Halloween costume. We stopped by the house earlier to pick up the diaper bag we left the last time we were there and got the grand tour of Zak's decorations. I have to say, they're really something. He must have spent hours getting everything into place."

"He's been working on the design since the beginning of October," I verified. "I especially love the life-size Frankenstein and Mrs. Frankenstein at the front door. They can be set to speak to you when you come in, but I have that part turned off for now. It was making the dogs crazy, plus it's a little creepy if you come in alone after dark."

"With all those orange globes you have, I'm not sure how you can see the dark for all the light."

"Tell me about it. I had to make him put them on a timer so they weren't shining in our faces when we went to bed."

"So far the only decoration we have is a pumpkin for the front porch. I think that in this case less is more, and up until today, I was pretty sure your dad felt the same way. But after seeing all Zak's electronics, I'm half-expecting to wake up to a decorating nightmare."

I laughed. "What is it about boys and their toys?"

"Every time I point out to your dad that perhaps he doesn't need to get every electronic device his future son-in-law has, he reminds me that I have an entire closet dedicated to shoes."

It occurred to me that this was the first time Mom had referred to Zak as her future son-in-law. I wasn't sure how I felt about that, since we weren't even officially engaged. On the other hand, I guess everyone realized it was only a matter of time.

"Your dad and I were going to head over to the snack shack and get a couple of burgers. Do you want to join us? You too, Ellie."

"Thanks, but we're going to wait to eat with our dates." Ellie actually blushed, which was weird because she'd been dating like crazy and everyone knew it.

"Well, you girls have a nice time," Dad said as he kissed me on the cheek before leading Mom and Harper away.

"Oh, there's Peter coming from the parking lot," Ellie informed me. "Save our place in line and I'll go to meet him."

I grinned as Ellie jogged away. She really was in to this guy. I just hoped he was as super as he seemed. I wasn't sure that a relationship would work out for them in the long run since he lived in the valley and she owned a business at the lake, but it would be nice if she found someone nice to hang out with in the short term.

"I spy with my little eye the fairest maiden in all the land." Zak jogged up behind me and scooped me into his arms.

"Zak, you nut, put me down."

"Not unless you know the magic phrase," he teased.

I whispered something in his ear.

He smiled. "That's not what I had in mind, but it will do." He set me on my feet.

"I thought you had another half hour at the snack bar."

"A couple of the guys scheduled for the second shift showed up early, so I decided to see if my princess was in need of rescue. Are you? In need of rescue?"

"Not at the moment, but *you* might be if you keep calling me princess."

"Oh, I do love them sassy."

"You are such a jerk."

"Maybe, but I'm an excellent kisser." And he kissed me to prove his point.

I couldn't help but smile at his playful mood. Zak was almost never in a bad mood, but he did tend to be more serious than silly. Maybe the Halloween spirit had gotten him in touch with his inner child. Whatever the reason for his playful mood, I liked it.

"Dad said he came by the house earlier. I guess you've given him the decorating bug. Mom said he's itching to keep up now that he saw all your electronics."

"He can try to catch up, but I am the *decorator.*" Zak said that last word in the same way someone might say *terminator*.

I laughed. "I think you have Halloween on the brain."

"I thought it was your favorite holiday."

"It is."

"So why aren't *you* going a little Halloween crazy?"

"I'm crazy, just not as crazy as you. How about we check out the maze after the hayride? Just you and me," I suggested. "We can hide in the shadows and make out."

"Why don't we go home to make out and save the maze for tomorrow?"

"An even better idea."

"By the way, Levi stopped by the snack bar. He and Darla aren't going to join us. He thought things might be a little weird between Darla and Ellie."

I was sorry Levi wasn't meeting us, but it was probably just as well. Ellie was on a date of sorts—a first date—and the added tension of the Ellie/Levi dynamic might give Peter the wrong impression. Or I guess it would actually be the right impression, but perhaps not the one she'd want to make right out of the gate.

"Zak, this is Peter; Peter, Zak," Ellie introduced the guys when she returned with Peter on her arm.

"So how is Shep doing?" Peter asked Ellie once the introductions had been made.

"He's settling in nicely. He loves having the lake in his backyard to romp around."

"I'll bet."

"If you'd like to see him, you can come by the boathouse after the hayride," Ellie offered.

"I'd like that."

I looked at Zak and winked. We both recognized the smooth way she'd gotten him to come back to her place. Or maybe he was the one with the smooth moves? Either way, I was certain I was witnessing a romance in the making.

By the time we got to the front of the line, it was completely dark, which added a whole other level to the event. Riding through the dense forest at night, with all the nocturnal animals rustling about in the shrubs, was spooky even without the actors dressed as ghosts who floated around in the woods as the wagons traversed the narrow dirt trail. I was impressed by how many automated props Joel had managed to set up in the short amount of time he'd had to prepare.

I snuggled close to Zak for both warmth and security. It seemed that Peter and Ellie had had a similar idea. I was glad to see that Ellie had finally hooked up with a guy with genuine potential.

I suppressed a scream when a headless horseman came riding up wielding a sword. The live actors really added a sense of the terrifying to the event. I was pretty sure the man in the horseman costume was my dentist, but even with that knowledge, I found my heart pounding as he threatened to take the head of anyone who passed through the woods.

"That was really fun," I said when the wagon had returned us safely to the staging area. "Anyone up for a drink?"

"I think Peter and I are going to head back to the boathouse," Ellie informed me. "I hate to leave Shep alone for too long. Catch up with you tomorrow?"

"Have fun." I grinned.

"You know," I reached up to wrap my arms around Zak's neck after they'd gone, "I bet Charlie and Bella are lonely too."

"Then I think we should definitely go home and check on them." Zak grabbed my hand and we started toward the truck. "I left a bottle of champagne to chill in case we decided we wanted to take a late-night dip in the spa."

"Champagne? That sounds . . . oh shoot." I stopped walking.

"We have a problem?"

"I forgot that I promised Tawny I'd cover the final two hours of her shift at the haunted maze. Her babysitter needed to leave early. Rain check on the champagne?"

# Chapter 9

## Saturday, October 25

The worst thing about the zombie run is that it always starts very early in the morning after a very late night. Last year Zak had arrived early and gotten everything set up before I even showed up, and this year was no different. When my alarm went off a full hour after the time I'd originally set it for, I found a note from him where his warm body should have been, letting me know that he was heading over early to set things up and that the coffee was on the timer and an egg pie was warming in the oven.

Have I mentioned that I have the best boyfriend *ever*?

"Ellie's not here?" I asked after eating my breakfast, showering, and driving to the starting point of the run.

"I haven't seen her," Zak answered after he kissed me good morning.

"I guess she might have had a late night with Peter. Do we have enough volunteers to man all the stations?"

"I think we're covered. Levi is going over last-minute instructions with the zombies and Darla is manning the sign-in table for the runners. I have all the electronic equipment set up, and a couple of cheerleaders showed up with the football players Levi recruited to play the zombies, so I have them giving out numbers and T-shirts. We should be good to go. Did you decide to leave Charlie at home?"

"Yeah, he was curled up with Bella. I made them go out before I left, but they both seemed pretty content to go back to sleep. I miss having Charlie with me as much as I used to, but I think he enjoys hanging out with Bella part of the time."

"I bet dogs like spending time with other dogs the same way people like spending time with people."

"I know there's *one* people I like to spend time with." I stood on tiptoe and gave Zak a quick kiss on the cheek. "I missed waking up to you."

"I figured you'd prefer to sleep in a bit."

"You figured right, but I have to say I'm quite enjoying this cohabitation thing."

Zak smiled.

"I guess I should head over and make sure the runners know the rules."

"I'm pretty sure Levi has that handled," Zak assured me. "You might want to check with the cheerleaders, though."

I looked toward the table where the four young girls were talking and laughing. Sometimes it seems like a million years since I was in high school and my biggest goal was to get an invitation to the homecoming dance and my biggest fear was that I wouldn't. Of course, all the high-school students at the race today were either jocks or cheerleaders, so I was pretty certain all of their dating needs were taken care of.

"Who is that talking to Paul?" I asked.

Paul Iverson, the newest member of the events committee and the new director for the summer camp in the area since Frank Valdez had been arrested for attempting to rob the bank the previous spring, was standing near the registration booth talking to a man I didn't recognize.

"I'm not sure," Zak answered. "They arrived together a little while ago. I overheard a bit of their conversation and got the impression that the man is somehow involved with the camp, either as a volunteer or an investor. I suppose the man could even be a parent, although they were talking about long-range consequences of one sort or another. It looks like Levi is getting the runners lined up; I should head over. I'll meet you at the finish line."

"Okay, and thanks again for getting up early and getting everything handled."

"No problem. It's what awesome boyfriends do."

"You didn't take a quiz in a men's magazine, did you?"

Zak just smiled as he walked away.

I looked back toward where Paul was speaking to the man I'd noticed before. I was certain I didn't recognize him, but I felt the familiar tingling I often do when trouble is brewing. The man looked to be in his early- to midthirties. He wasn't dressed like a businessman, so perhaps he was a volunteer or even a parent. Of course, it was early on a Saturday morning. Maybe investor types didn't even dress like investors at that hour. I was debating about whether to go over and introduce myself when Darla waved me to the sign-in table, where a late arrival was demanding to be allowed to participate even though the race was seconds from starting. I would have liked to assuage my curiosity about the man Paul was speaking to, but when duty calls, it's only polite to answer.

"How can I help?" I asked as I approached the sign-in table.

"I'm running a little late, but I'd still like to participate," a man dressed as a zombie answered.

"The race has already started, but if you run real fast, I guess you can try to catch up."

"Thanks." The man took off running at a pace that was never going to catch him up to the others, but if he didn't mind running the race a good quarter mile behind the pack, who was I to stop him?

I looked back toward the location where I'd seen Paul talking with the man I'd had a feeling was someone I should talk to. "Did you see where Paul went?" I asked Darla.

"He headed toward the parking area. I think he was leaving."

"Do you know who that was he was talking to?"

"No, he didn't say, but I got the feeling the guy was from out of the area. When he arrived, Paul looked surprised to see him. He went right over and shook his hand, so I assume they know each other from before today."

"Did Paul say anything at all that might indicate who he was or where he knew him from?" I asked.

Darla frowned. "Why? Do you know him?"

"No. I just have a feeling I might have seen him somewhere before."

Darla shrugged. "Paul didn't say much at all, really. We were talking, he looked up and saw the man, said something like 'what is he doing here?' and then walked over and started talking to him. If you want to know who he is, I guess you can call Paul."

"I just might do that."

After the zombie run wrapped up, Zak and I headed back into town to have some lunch and attend the kiddie carnival. Hazel and the other members of the events committee who'd helped decorate the community center had done a wonderful job. Children of all ages, most dressed in costume, were dispersed around the room, playing the twenty or so games the committee had come up with. The lines wound through the room as tykes tossed beanbags through the face of a giant jack-o'-lantern made of plywood or rolled plastic bowling balls at plastic pins. The longest line of all, much to my surprise, was the fishing booth, where the participants cast strings attached to a pole over a blanket hung on a line in the hopes of catching prizes.

"Do you remember doing this when you were a kid?" I asked Zak as I watched the mother of a couple of little boys who were standing in line wrestle with a toddler who had other ideas.

"No, I don't think my parents ever brought me to a kiddie carnival when I was growing up."

I looked at Zak with pity. "Not even when you were little?"

"My parents didn't really go in for the whole play thing. Our family outings tended to be educational in nature. We'd go to museums or lectures at the university."

I scrunched my face in disgust. "You never even went to the carnivals they held when you were in elementary school?"

"Nope. I went to a private school until Mom and I moved here when I was in the seventh grade, and by that time I was really too old for kiddie carnivals."

"Come on." I grabbed Zak's hand and led him toward the dart toss. "You have to play at least one game. It's not natural to go your whole life without ever throwing a dart at a balloon."

I thought Zak might argue that he was too old for the kiddie games, but he just smiled as I led him across the room. Of course, he was way overqualified, so he won one of the big stuffed animals in no time, but Zak being Zak, he handed Willa a couple of large bills as a donation to the cause and then gave the stuffed giraffe to a little girl who had been trying to win her own toy the entire time we'd been there. Based on the adoration in her eyes when Zak handed her the giraffe, I was pretty sure the six-year-old had a new love in her life.

"That was fun," Zak announced as we walked toward the park where the pumpkin-carving competition was taking place. "When we have kids we'll be sure to take them to every carnival within a fifty-mile radius."

"It looks like a good turnout for the big event." I decided to ignore Zak's comment about *our* kids as we made our way through the crowd. Not that I didn't want kids someday, but to be honest, thinking about them made my hands sweat.

"How many entrants do we have this year?" Zak asked.

"I'm not sure. Let's head over to find out."

In Ashton Falls, we take our pumpkin carving seriously. Not only is each creation judged on its merit within the category in which it's entered, but overall size and presentation are taken into consideration as well. The self-titled "king" of pumpkin carving in town is Gunnar Rivers, one of the twin brothers who work for me at the Zoo covering the night shift. Gunnar has won Best Pumpkin Overall the last three years in a row, and six of the past ten.

Gunnar's brother, Tank, is a close contender. I believe it's the rivalry between the two that fuels the long hours they put into choosing the perfect design and carving every detail until it's just right. I'm fond of both brothers and have shown my support for both of their efforts, but secretly, I hope Tank wins this year because I understand the pain of coming in second year after year, no matter how hard you try.

Long tables had been set up around the gazebo in the park. Each contestant was assigned a table where he or she was allowed a half hour before the competition to set up. The actual carving of the entry was timed, but I knew after watching both Gunnar and Tank prepare that they'd carved many practice pumpkins with the design they'd selected in advance.

The entries were usually intricate carvings that in no way resembled the jack-o'-lanterns with three triangles and a crooked mouth that are my specialty. After the contest, the artful gourds are displayed on tables that had been set up inside the gazebo. In addition to the official ranking set by the judges, spectators were given the opportunity to vote for their favorite, and a people's choice ribbon was presented at the end of the day. In my experience, the winning of this particular ribbon tended to be more of a popularity contest than a contest of skill.

"It looks like there are twelve people entered," I commented as I counted the number of pumpkins that were set out, waiting to be carved.

"Looks like a competitive pool."

"Gunnar is pretty certain he'll win, but I wouldn't mind seeing someone else. I know he's been practicing; he'll be hard to beat."

"How come you don't do a pumpkin?" Zak asked.

I shrugged. "Too busy. Maybe you should enter next year."

"Maybe I will."

I looked around the crowd to see if I could catch a glimpse of Ellie or Levi, both of whom should have been in the area. I didn't see either of my friends, but I did spot someone else.

"There's the man I saw talking to Paul this morning. I'm going to go over and start up a conversation with him."

"Remind me why you want to talk to him?" Zak asked.

"I'm not sure; I just know that my Zodar went off this morning when I saw him. I really don't know why, but I figure it can't hurt to head over and say hi."

"Okay, let's go." Zak took my hand and led me across the park.

I tried to figure out whether I knew the man from somewhere. He seemed familiar, and yet he didn't. He could just be a visitor I'd come across in passing, but somehow I didn't think so. There was this nagging memory in the back of my mind that couldn't quite make its way to the surface.

"I'm sorry; do I know you?" I began after approaching the man.

Zak looked at me and rolled his eyes. Okay, so I'm not really all that proficient at starting conversations.

"My girlfriend, Zoe, saw you at the zombie run this morning and thought she recognized you from somewhere," Zak added.

"I'm sorry, but I don't recognize you." The man smiled. "My name is Drake Bollington."

Drake Bollington was the name of one of the counselors who had been at the Henderson house party.

"Actually, when I saw you this morning, I thought you seemed familiar, but now I realize I must have just recognized you from your photo."

"Photo?" the man asked.

"I have a friend who has a photo of the counselors who were employed at the summer camp he worked at one year. When you mentioned your name, I put two and two together. You worked at that camp the year all those people died," I continued. "I guess you heard that Adam Davenport was also back in town. Or at least he was."

Drake's face became guarded. "I heard Adam was in the area. I guess he had an accident."

"He was murdered."

I watched the man's face. He didn't get defensive at my bold statement, but he didn't seem surprised either.

"I know we just met, but I was wondering if you would mind filling me in on some of the details of the night in question."

The man glared at me. He appeared to check me out before answering. Not that I blamed him; my delivery was just a tad awkward.

"Why are you interested in finding out about that night?" he asked. "You a cop?"

I shook my head. "No, just an interested party. I've been doing some research into the events of that evening. Talking to people; that sort of thing. I guess uncovering mysteries is sort of a hobby of mine."

"I don't know you, so to be honest, I'm not all that comfortable having this conversation. I'm sorry, but I really have to go."

"My name is Zoe Donovan," I added as the man turned to leave. "Ask Paul about me, if that would make you feel more comfortable. I work at the Zoo, an animal rehabilitation shelter in town. Call me there anytime. If I'm not on the premises, one of my employees will be able to tell you how to get hold of me. And I'm really not a cop. Like I said, I'm just an interested party."

The man frowned and walked away.

"I think you might need to work on your interrogation skills," Zak commented.

I shrugged. "I accomplished what I intended. I found out who he is, gave him something to think about, and told him how to get hold of me. He'll call."

"You seem certain about that."

"I am. He's as curious about what I know as I am about what he knows. If he's involved in what happened at the Henderson house, he'll want to know what I know. He just needs some time to think it through. He'll call when he's ready."

# Chapter 10

## Monday, October 27

I decided to head to the Zoo early on Monday morning. Between the Haunted Hamlet the previous weekend and the murder investigation, I was behind on my paperwork. I knew that Jeremy would take up the slack if I asked him, but I really love my job and have missed spending time with the animals I've vowed to serve.

Of the eight kittens we'd acquired the previous week, six had been adopted. I decided to let the two that were still with us have some extra people time, so I took them out of their cage to play on the floor of my office while I sorted through the pile of mail I'd acquired over the past few days. I hoped the kittens would find homes sooner rather than later. They were fuzzy and pure black, with huge blue eyes and the sweetest personalities, and they were working their way into my heart. If too much more time went by, I'd probably end up bringing them home, and even I knew that the last thing I needed were more pets.

I tossed a fuzzy toy mouse onto the floor and watched as the boys bravely attacked it. They really were adorable. Returning my attention to the pile of mail in front of me, I noticed that I had a pink slip from Mr. Hanover, letting me know that he had stopped in the previous Friday with a certified letter he needed me to sign for. It was most likely the operating contract the county had insisted on modifying, in spite of the fact that the old contract was perfectly fine. The slip said he'd attempt to deliver the envelope again today, and if I was still unavailable, I'd need to pick up the letter from the post office.

Mr. Hanover usually came by first thing in the morning, so it was likely I'd be on site when he arrived.

"You're here early," Tiffany greeted me as she walked into my office from the front of the building.

I motioned to the mess on my desk. "I have a lot of paperwork to catch up on, so I decided to get an early start."

"Did Tank leave already?" Tiffany asked.

"Yeah. I told him he could go ahead and take off since I was here. He was pretty excited about winning the pumpkin-carving competition yesterday. Talk about a good mood. He was still walking on air."

Tiffany laughed. "Yeah, well, just wait until Gunnar shows up tonight. I have a feeling we'll be exposed to a different mood entirely."

"It's too bad for our sake they both couldn't win." I smiled.

"It would make life easier. I see you've freed Trick and Treat from their cages."

"Trick and Treat?" I asked as I looked toward the kittens who were both sitting on the windowsill, looking out.

"It seemed appropriate. It is Halloween, and they *are* black cats."

"Yeah, I guess Trick and Treat are appropriate names. Which is which?"

Tiffany shrugged. "It doesn't matter. I figure whoever adopts them will give them new names anyway. Although I do hope the little guys get adopted together. They're from the same litter and really seem to have bonded."

"Let me think about it. Maybe I can come up with someone to take them both."

"I can't have animals in my apartment or I'd take them myself. As soon as I can afford to, I'm going to move to a building that allows pets."

"Be careful or you'll end up with a house full like me."

Tiffany laughed. "You're probably right. I guess I'll head back and start exercising the dogs."

I returned to my paperwork as Trick and Treat continued to romp around the room. If I was going to find someone to take the brothers, I was going to need to find someone who enjoyed the high energy two kittens created when allowed to play together. One kitten would more often than not spend a good part of the day sleeping, but two . . . two could be a fun and delightful handful.

Zak had taken both dogs for a run that morning but planned to bring Charlie and Bella with him when he came by later in the day to work on the new pens we were building. It seemed as if new pen construction was an ongoing event; our facility was becoming well known as the place to take wildlife in need of rehabilitation or temporary housing. The bear cubs we had been nurturing for almost a year were ready to be released into the dens we'd picked out for them. Hopefully they'd settle in and hibernate before the heavy snow arrived in a month or so.

"Mr. Hanover is here to see you." Jeremy poked his head in the doorway shortly after Tiffany had left.

"I'll be right out."

I set the stack of mail I was holding down on my desk and stood up. I made sure the kittens were content and safely napping before I snuck out of the room, closing the door behind me. I would only be a few minutes, but I certainly didn't want them to escape. The last thing we needed was Halloween kittens terrorizing the building.

"Mr. Hanover," I greeted as I walked into the reception area. "It's so nice to see you. You have a letter for me?"

"I do, but you'll need ID and a signature to get it."

"You've known me since I was a kid," I pointed out.

"Rules are rules, and the rules say that I need to see some ID."

"My purse is in my office. If you can wait just a minute, I'll get it."

"I can come back to your office. I wouldn't mind sittin' for a spell while we complete our business. My old legs don't get around as well as they used to."

"I'd be happy to have you take your break in my office, but I have to warn you that I have kittens in there. Two of them. Lively little guys who might see fit to attack your feet while you walk or pounce on your head while you sit."

Mr. Hanover smiled. "I love kittens. My Genevieve passed a while back, and I've missed having a cat to come home to."

"Okay, great. Come on back. Can I get you some coffee?"

"That would be nice."

I escorted Mr. Hanover into my office before heading back to the lounge to pour him some coffee. I'd been hesitant to introduce him to the boys, who could be rather rambunctious when they weren't peacefully sleeping, but by the time I returned, he had both kittens sitting on his lap, purring away like the little angels I knew they weren't.

"I sure do miss having a cat on my lap," Mr. Hanover said again. "I don't suppose the boys are still available?"

I hesitated. "They are, but we wanted to try to adopt them together, if possible."

"I'd be willing to take them both," Mr. Hanover offered.

"Really? I know they seem all sweet and angelic at the moment, but they can be a handful. Once they get to chasing each other around the room, it's a total free-for-all."

Mr. Hanover picked up one of the kittens and looked him in the eye. "You gonna give me any trouble?"

The kitten batted at Mr. Hanover's long nose with his paw.

"I think the boys and I will be fine. If they're available, that is. I'm being forced to retire, even though I have a good ten years left in me. I could use the company."

"Okay, then," I said. "We'll arrange for a trial adoption. If you find they're too much for you, we'll happily take them back. If they work out okay, we can complete the paperwork in a week or two. You'll want to have them neutered. I'll make the arrangements when you're ready."

Mr. Hanover smiled. "That's wonderful. I guess I *was* able to pull a little magic out of my last day on the job."

"This is your last day? I didn't realize."

I felt bad for the guy. On one hand, the man should have retired years ago. On the other, the post office was his life. I hated to think of him home alone with no purpose. Of course, now that he had Trick and Treat to keep him company, his days would be filled with kitty shenanigans.

"I have your letter right here." Mr. Hanover handed it to me.

"Do you still need to see that ID?"

"Naw. Guess I never really did. I just wanted an excuse to sit for a spell. Can I come back for the kittens after my shift?"

"Certainly. I'll get some supplies together for you. I should be here most of the day, now that the Haunted Hamlet is over, but if I'm not here for some reason, either Jeremy or Tiffany can help you get loaded up."

"I took a spin on that hayride that was substituted for the haunted barn. It was a lot more fun than I expected, though I'm not sure it will work as a permanent option due to our finicky weather."

"Yes, the committee thought of that. We knew the weather was supposed to hold through the weekend, but I hear we have a storm coming in later today. I'm sure we'll look for another indoor venue next year. We've had to cancel the haunted maze several times in the past, so we can't risk having a second outdoor event. We got lucky with the hayride after what happened."

"I heard about the man who died in the house," Mr. Hanover commented. "I've been in that house, you know."

"You have?"

"Yup. When I was younger. A couple of friends and I snuck in to check out the secret room when that spooky old owner was away for a few days."

"Secret room?"

"There's a panel leading to a room at the back of the attic. Most folks don't even know it's there. You really don't notice it unless you're looking for it, and then you can't open it unless you know the secret."

"The secret?"

When Zak showed up with Charlie and Bella, I filled him in on everything Mr. Hanover had told me about the secret room. I had to admit I was intrigued. I wondered if the room somehow played into the mysterious deaths thirteen years earlier. After a bit of a discussion, Zak agreed to accompany me to check it out. At least this time, I figured, it would still be totally light, and we had two brave guard dogs with us.

The problem with that scenario, I quickly realized, was that the storm had already blown in, bringing not only a heavy darkness but rain, thunder, and lightning as well.

"If I was watching a movie where a couple and their dogs were on their way to a haunted house in a lightning storm four days before Halloween, I'd think they were nuts," I commented as Zak swerved to avoid a large tree branch in the road.

"Are you sure you want to do this now?" Zak asked as he slowly maneuvered his truck through the obstacle course created by the heavy wind and pounding rain.

Was I? It made more sense to wait until the storm passed. "We're almost there. We might as well go in and check it out. If we don't find anything, we'll still have a funny story to tell our grandchildren."

Zak glanced at me. "Grandchildren?"

Saying that we'd have a story for our grandchildren was a commonly used phrase. I didn't mean that we'd necessarily have grandchildren together. Did I? If we married, then having children would be the natural progression of things, and children more often than not led to grandchildren, but I didn't think I was quite ready to have this particular discussion with Zak.

"Metaphorical grandchildren," I answered. "Look out for that dog."

Zak swerved to avoid a small dog that had run in front of us and then cowered behind a large evergreen shrub.

"Pull over," I directed.

Zak pulled the truck to the side of the road.

"I'm pretty sure we missed him. I think he ran into those bushes." I started to open my door.

"Stay here," Zak directed. "I'll get him."

Zak pulled the hood of his sweatshirt over his head as he dashed into the rain. It really was coming down. The poor guy was going to be drenched by the time he convinced the frightened dog to come back to the truck with him.

Bella whined as she looked out the window at Zak. It was sweet that she had already bonded with him to the point where she was concerned about him. Of course, what I took for concern might just have been discontent that he'd gotten out of the truck and hadn't taken her with him. In spite of the fact that she was a big dog and not all that young, she followed Zak around like a puppy.

I was just about to get out and assist Zak when he started back toward the truck with the pup in his arms. At first glance, I thought the dog was older, of a small breed, but upon closer examination, I could see he was clearly a puppy.

"Poor baby," I cooed as Zak placed the puppy in my arms and Bella greeted Zak with wet doggie kisses.

A large lightning strike flashed through the sky. "Maybe we should just come back tomorrow," I suggested. "This poor little guy seems to be scared to death. I'd like to get him home, fed, and settled in for the night."

"Yeah, maybe that's a good idea," Zak agreed. "The secret passage isn't going anywhere. If there are clues there now, they should still be there tomorrow."

The drive back to the house was tricky; Zak had to swerve to avoid pinecones and small branches that had broken away from the trees that lined the road. Lightning streaked through the dark sky, followed by claps of thunder that echoed off the surrounding mountains. Then, as we approached the highway, the sky opened up, making driving impossible.

Zak pulled the truck over to the side of the road until the downpour let up. The puppy in my arms was shaking in fear as lightning streaked around us. Charlie climbed over the seat and snuggled up next to me. Bella was too big to fit in the front, so Zak scratched her head where she rested it on his shoulder and spoke softly to her as we waited out the worst of the storm.

After we arrived at the house, I dried and fed the dogs while Zak built a fire in the large stone fireplace in his cozy kitchen. Once the puppy realized he was safe with us, he began to explore. When the dogs were settled in front of the fire, Zak and I changed into warm, dry clothes.

Although it wasn't all that late, neither of us felt much like making dinner, so Zak heated up some leftover soup while I called Gunnar, who was on duty at the Zoo that night, to see if anyone had called to report a missing puppy. Chances were the thunder had scared the little guy, who had taken off running and ended up lost.

"No one has called to report a missing puppy, but Gunnar said he'd call if someone does," I informed Zak, who set a bowl of broccoli cheese soup in front of me, along with a biscuit from the batch he'd whipped up while the soup heated.

The rain continued to fall in sheets, but the lightning seemed to have passed, allowing Bella, Charlie, and our temporary houseguest to drift off into a dreamless sleep in front of the fire. At least I guessed it was dreamless. I don't suppose I actually knew if they were dreaming or not, but they seemed content and restful, and dreamless seemed a poetic way to describe it. Marlow and Spade were both curled up in the window seat next to the fire, enjoying the warmth while creating a bit of distance between themselves and the new puppy in the house.

"I guess it's a good thing we decided to check out the Henderson house or this poor little guy might have had to spend the night out in the storm," I commented.

"There aren't any houses in the area where we found him," Zak said. "I wonder where he came from."

"I wish I knew. Hopefully, he was simply lost, not abandoned. He does feel pretty skinny, like he hasn't eaten for a while, and I'm afraid this wouldn't be the first time I found a dog or cat that had simply been abandoned by their owner."

The lights flickered as a gust of wind hit the side of the house. Although the lake outside the large picture window in Zak's kitchen was usually calm, waves at least five feet high had been created by the wind and sent crashing onto the sandy beach. It felt like we were at the ocean rather than the lake.

"Maybe we should gather some candles and a couple of flashlights," I suggested. "If the storm doesn't let up, I'd be willing to bet we'll lose power by the end of the evening."

"Good idea. I have a couple of flashlights in that drawer by the door, and there's a bunch of candles in the storage closet upstairs."

"It's really cozy in here with the storm and the fire." I placed my hand over Zak's, which was resting on the dining table where we'd been eating.

Zak squeezed my hand. "It is cozy. After we eat, I think I'll start a fire in both the living room and the bedroom. I have wood stacked on the enclosed service porch, so it'll be easy to keep them going, and they'll provide warmth in case the heat goes out."

"Plus it's romantic."

"Yeah," Zak grinned, "there's that as well."

Zak got up to clear the table, waking the puppy, who wandered over to sit at my feet. If I had to guess, I'd say he was a lab mix of some sort. He was a beautiful charcoal gray not commonly found in labs, but his short hair, big eyes, and floppy ears gave him a lablike quality. It was hard to tell his exact age, but I thought he was three or four months old. I picked him up and walked into the living room, where Zak was working on the fire. I put him down on the sofa next to me and then covered him with the afghan I'd tossed to one side that morning.

"Do you think we should give him a name?" I asked Zak, who was fanning the flame as the pup settled in and laid his head on my leg.

"Honestly, I think giving him a name is a bad idea. He probably has a human who's looking for him, so it's best not to get too attached."

I sighed. "You're right. It really is a miracle I don't have fifty dogs and fifty cats with all the sweet things that pass through the Zoo. There were two black kittens at the Zoo that had latched onto my heart before Mr. Hanover saved me by adopting them."

"I heard today was his last day at the post office," Zak commented as Bella and Charlie wandered in from the kitchen and lay down at our feet.

"Yeah, that's what he said. It seemed odd that his last day would be on a Monday, but apparently he negotiated an extra day to make the rounds and say his good-byes. It seems they sprang it on him last Friday, when he came in from his route."

"You'd think they would have given him notice."

I agreed. "I suppose they thought doing it quickly would be less painful. Mr. Hanover said he'll be well taken care of financially."

"I'm glad Mr. Hanover got hooked up with the kittens," Zak commented. "Not that they wouldn't have been welcome here if you'd decided to adopt them, but perhaps having their company will help him with the transition."

"That's what I thought as well. Have you heard how long this storm is supposed to hang around?"

"I think it's supposed to blow through by morning," Zak answered.

"I'm afraid you're going to have to spend a good part of tomorrow redecorating after the wind finishes undoing everything you've done."

"I figured as much." Zak got up to stir the fire. "We can go out to the Henderson house in the morning and then I'll come back to start on the cleanup. I'm sure the beach will be a mess too. It seems like we always get a lot of garbage washing up after a storm."

A clap of thunder shook the house, and the lights flickered and then went out. Both Bella and Charlie jumped on the sofa with us.

"It looks like we're going to have a full bed tonight," I said as I cuddled with the frightened dogs.

# Chapter 11

## Tuesday, October 28

Zak and I headed back to the Henderson house first thing the next morning. The rain had stopped sometime during the night, but the roads were flooded in many low-lying areas, and the debris left by the strong winds created an obstacle course worthy of a race-car driver. Zak drove carefully as he maneuvered around tree branches and large boulders that had washed down the gully.

"I'm glad I wore my work boots," I commented as we parked in front of the house and I stepped down out of the truck and into the mud.

Zak and I walked hand in hand across the dirt drive, up the rotted steps, and into the musty entry. Unlike my other visits, this time I knew exactly where I was headed. We quickly made our way through the downstairs living area and up the stairs to the second floor. I paused as we passed the spot where we had found Davenport's body. Hopefully, he was the only victim of the spooky old house. We headed toward the steps leading to the attic. With each step, I felt the knot in my stomach tense just a little bit tighter.

The door to the attic was firmly shut. I supposed the hinges must have rusted with age because it took all of Zak's might to create a passageway large enough for us to squeeze through. The attic was dark and stuffy and filled with boxes of assorted sizes.

"There must be a hundred years' worth of dust up here," Zak said as we began to search the far wall for the hidden lever Mr. Hanover had told me about.

"I know. It's creepy to think that all of this stuff has been up here for so long. I wonder what's in all these boxes."

"Probably junk. If there was anything of value, I imagine someone would have made off with it before now."

"Maybe. Although with all the weird stuff that's happened in this house, I doubt there've been that many prowlers lurking about. I think I found something," I said as my hand encountered a board that had a small amount of give to it. As instructed by Mr. Hanover, I pushed firmly on the board and then held it down until a small door popped open.

"It's really dark," Zak commented as he poked his head into the windowless room.

I turned on my flashlight and slowly inched into the narrow passage. The room was really a long, narrow hallway that seemed to border the outline of the house. I couldn't imagine why anyone would have built such a room, but I suddenly realized how someone could have rigged lamps and furniture to fly through the air thirteen years ago. It would probably be easy to control objects from above with the right technology.

"I see something ahead," I whispered as I stopped walking.

"What is it?" Zak asked from behind me. He had to walk stooped over due to the combination of his extreme height and the low ceiling of the passage.

"It looks like a body. A real one. We'd better call Salinger."

I know I've said this before, but I think it warrants saying again: sometimes I really do hate being right. The skeleton in the secret room had been there for quite some time. Based on the STAR LAKE CAMP COUNSELOR dog tag around the neck, I was willing to bet that our victim was none other than missing counselor Bart Coleman. Lying next to him was an old video camera. It had been damaged, and I wasn't certain the film would be any good after sitting in the attic all these years.

"Maybe the camera can tell us something," I suggested.

"Guess I can send it down to the county offices." Salinger sighed. "We don't really have anyone on staff who knows much about this sort of thing."

"I can try to see what I can do with it," Zak offered.

Salinger hesitated. I knew he hated to get us involved. He always resisted, yet Zak and I always seemed to end up in the thick of things.

"Okay, if you think you can get a look at the film, that will be helpful. Let me know what you find."

"So what are we going to do about our little hitchhiker from last night?" Zak asked as we drove back toward the house. "Do you want to take him to the Zoo?"

"I'd like to keep him at the house for now. He's been through enough, and he seems to have latched onto Bella. I think I'll have Scott check him over to make sure he's totally healthy, and then I'll let Jeremy know to keep his eye out for the right human for the little guy."

"What about Ethan? You mentioned that you were keeping an eye out for a dog for him."

"I don't think Ethan has the energy a young dog would need. I'd like to find him an adult dog, or perhaps a smaller dog with lower exercise needs. I know this pup has been really mellow since we've had him, but I think that's the result of being a bit insecure with his situation. Once he gets settled in, I'd be willing to bet he'll be hell on wheels. I need a loving and caring human who has both the patience and energy to raise a young lab."

All three dogs greeted us at the door when we arrived home. You'd think we'd been gone for days rather than just a few hours. We let the dogs run around on the beach for a bit before bringing them back inside. The worst thing about the sand-and-dog combination is that vacuuming becomes a full-time activity.

"Whoever killed Bart Coleman—assuming the victim turns out to be Bart Coleman—has to have known about the secret room," I theorized as Zak put away the dog food we had stopped to pick up. "I'm not a hundred percent certain of this, but it seems that there are probably very few people who know about the room. It's not like it stands out. You pretty much need to know it's there to find it."

"Mr. Hanover said that when he broke into the house to check out the room, he went with a couple of buddies, so there were at least two other people who knew about the room. The way boys trend to brag, I'd say they filled in others after their trip into the spooky house."

"True. I guess I should have thought about the gossip factor. This whole thing is giving me a headache. I think I'm going to head into town. Do you want to come?"

"Actually, I think I'll stay here and work on the film. Why don't you bring home some Chinese food and we can watch another one of those cheesy horror movies you like? It's only three days until Halloween."

"How about something with Boris Karloff?"

"Karloff sounds good."

Every Tuesday for the past five years, I've attended the Ashton Falls Event Committee meeting. Well, almost every Tuesday. I've missed a few over the years, and I was planning to skip this week, but I decided to show up even if I would be late. Ellie had mentioned that Willa was planning to hand out assignments for both the Thanksgiving dinner and the Christmas Carnival at this week's meeting. The committee had a habit of assigning unpleasant tasks to committee members who were absent. The last time I missed the preholiday meeting, I ended up wearing tights and a pointy hat in Santa's Village for the entire carnival weekend, so I figured this wasn't a good meeting to miss.

"Oh good, Zoe's here," Willa said as I walked through the hallway that separated the back room from the main part of Rosie's Café. "We have a new member today, so I hoped everyone would be here."

"New member?" I asked.

"Zoe Donovan, I'd like you to meet Brooke Collins."

My heart sank as I looked at the woman sitting between Levi and my dad. Brooke Collins was not only the most stunningly beautiful woman I had ever met, but I had the sickening feeling she was none other than Zak's ex-girlfriend Brooke. The only reason I knew that he and this woman had once . . . I really couldn't think about that . . . was because he still carried a photo of her in his wallet.

"Zoe, how are you, dear? I've heard so much about you," Brooke greeted me like I was some sort of easily dismissed child.

"Really?"

"Zak mentioned that the two of you were dating the last time I spoke to him. I'm always happy to meet Zak's women."

*Zak's women?* I really had thought I'd put Jealous Zoe to bed once and for all, but when I looked at the tall blonde with legs that seemed to go on forever, I was pretty sure Jealous Zoe was alive and well.

"Brooke has been kind enough to bring her big-city fund-raising knowledge to our little village in an effort to help balance the budget, which is currently on life support," Willa added. It was obvious by Willa's smile that Brooke had at least one fan in the room.

"I thought the committee was for residents only," I pointed out.

Originally, the committee had been organized by a small group of residents who wanted to pool their resources to fund their specific projects. At the time, I worked for the county animal control, which was vastly underfunded and really needed the money we earned. Now Zak owns the Zoo and it's fully funded by his millions, but I remain on the committee to support the rest of the community and their pet projects.

"Brooke has informed me that she's in the process of moving to Ashton Falls," Willa all but gushed. "Isn't that wonderful?"

"Yeah, wonderful."

Ellie got up and grabbed another chair, which she set next to her own. She waved me over, indicating that I should take it.

"Now that we're *all* here," Willa emphasized, "I want to share with you our fabulous news."

"News?" I asked as I sat down beside Ellie.

"As you are all aware, the money the committee is able to earn through our events and the needs of those we try to serve have suffered a widening gap as of late. Brooke came to me with a suggestion that I think could make all the difference to next year's budget."

Ellie must have known what was coming because she squeezed my leg in warning.

"November has always been a money-loss month rather than a money-gain month for us," Willa began.

"The Thanksgiving dinner is something we do for the citizens of our community," I spoke up. "It isn't supposed to make money."

"I realize that." Willa scolded me with her eyes for interrupting. "However, with the increase in budget each nonprofit is asking for, I've been looking for the opportunity to turn that around. Luckily for the volunteer firefighters, library, and theater arts program, Brooke has come up with a wonderful idea."

I glanced at Ellie, who was digging her nails into my leg by this point. She gave me the "look," indicating that I should maintain my silence.

"Brooke has suggested that we open the dinner to the public, rather than limiting it to locals. If we do that, we can sell tickets, which should make us a nice profit."

"Why would anyone pay to come to our dinner?" I asked.

*Ouch.* I glared at Ellie, who had actually pinched me.

"Because," Brooke spoke up, "we're going to couple the dinner with a bachelor auction. Ashton Falls happens to be the home of one of the nation's most eligible bachelors, so I anticipate that the event will draw the sophisticates we need to make a killing."

I paled. They wanted to auction off Zak to the highest bidder? Brooke glared at me, and all at once I had a preview of who would end up with the winning bid. Maybe Zak making the top-ten bachelor list wasn't such a great thing after all.

"Of course," Brooke added, "we'll want to enlist the help of all of the eligible men in the area. You can't really have an auction with one prize. I have the connections to bring affluent women to the area, but you'll need to provide the men."

I was about to open my mouth when Ellie squeezed my hand so tight that it brought tears to my eyes.

"The last auction I attended with a participant from the top ten made over . . ." Brooke mentioned a number that made even my head spin.

"Everyone in favor of Brooke's idea?" Willa asked for a vote

"Aye," everyone in the room, including Ellie, agreed.

"Levi, Paul," Brooke looked directly at each of them in turn, "I'm assuming you'll participate?"

"Of course," both agreed.

"I figure we need at least ten men. Fifteen would be better," Brooke informed us. "With Zak we have three. Suggestions?"

"We don't know that Zak will agree to do this," I spoke up.

"Of course he will." Brooke laughed. "Zak is the most altruistic man I know. If it will benefit the community, he'll happily join in."

Brooke wasn't wrong. Zak probably would agree to the ridiculous idea if he felt it would help the community to buy the new fire engine we needed or books for the library.

"There are a couple of single firefighters I could probably talk into participating if it means a new truck," Dad spoke up.

*Traitor.*

"There are a few single men in the theater group as well," Gilda added.

I could barely sit still as the members of the committee sat around pimping out the single men of our community. There seemed to be only one solution. Zak and I would have to move.

My ex–best friend Ellie pulled me aside after the meeting. "I'm sorry, but it would've been worse if we didn't support the idea. The auction could make a huge difference to the community. You know how much we need a new engine for the volunteer firefighters, and we just talked last month about cutting funding to the summer camp and theater arts program altogether. We need this fund-raiser.

"Easy for you to say; your boyfriend doesn't live in Ashton Falls."

Ellie actually looked hurt. "First of all, Peter is not my boyfriend, and second of all, even if he was my boyfriend *and* he lived here, I'd be okay with his participating if it meant that Levi's afterschool sports program won't be cut and Tawny won't have to turn away preschoolers who are in need of scholarships. It's just for one night."

"Maybe, but you don't have America's biggest slut trying to steal your boyfriend."

"She isn't trying to steal Zak."

I just looked at Ellie.

"Okay, maybe she is, but she won't be successful. Zak loves you."

I knew Ellie was right. Zak did love me. Even if Brooke successfully bid on him, I knew I could trust him. "Yeah, I know you're right. I guess I just let Jealous Zoe get the better of me."

"You could always bid on him," Ellie suggested.

"I can't afford him."

"I guess you could always marry him."

I glanced at Ellie.

"I'm kidding. Marrying someone to prevent competition is the worst reason ever to get hitched."

"Yeah, I guess you're right. I guess I'll just have to start saving my money so I can buy the man I love."

"That's my girl." Ellie looped her arm though mine.

# Chapter 12

By the time I arrived at the Zoo, Jeremy and Tiffany had taken care of all of the routine chores. We talked about a possible placement for the pup Zak and I had found and all agreed we wanted to find the perfect human for the little guy if his owner couldn't be located. Scott was on his way out when I called him but agreed to stop by the house to take a quick look at our newest orphan at some point in the afternoon.

"Did Gunnar say how the animals did during the storm last night?" I asked.

"The wild animals didn't seem to mind it, and now that Trick and Treat have been adopted, we don't have any cats, so Gunnar let all the dogs sleep with him. When I came in this morning he was snoring away with all ten resident dogs either lying on him or next to him," Jeremy answered.

"Aw, that was so sweet of him. I'll have to be sure to thank him for going above and beyond."

"He seems to really care about the animals. Tank does as well. I think you made a good choice in hiring them. I hear we might be in for another storm tonight."

I looked out the window at the darkening sky. "Yeah, it looks like it."

"By the way," Jeremy continued, "Ellie came by yesterday to introduce me to Shep. He's a real beaut. I'm glad it worked out."

"It seems like he'll be a good fit for her, and she certainly has been happier since he came into her life."

"She mentioned that she's been out with Peter. He's a great guy, and you know I love Ellie, but I'm not sure about them as a couple. I hope she doesn't end up getting hurt again."

"I think she's taking things a bit more casually this time around. It's nice that you're concerned about her, though."

Jeremy shrugged. "We've become friends since she started hanging out with the single parents group. Even though she isn't dating a single parent anymore, she seems happy to babysit whenever anyone asks. Hopefully, she'll have her own little bundle someday."

"Hopefully. By the way, I spoke to the man who came in and wanted to adopt Jigger. I'm not sure he'll be the best match for the dog. Jigger has some pretty serious dominance issues, and the man I spoke to seemed timid, although he tried to appear like he was a tough guy. I'm afraid Jigger would walk all over him, so I suggested he take a look at the Great Dane that was brought in last week."

Jigger was a pit bull, and they tend to attract tough-guy types, but the reality is that many of them aren't all that tough at all. The Great Dane was large enough to appeal to a "real man" but was as gentle as a kitten.

"Did you get the feeling that the man otherwise qualified for one of our dogs?" Jeremy asked.

"Yeah, he seemed to really want a dog, and he's had them before. He has a large yard and his children are grown, so he lives along. He likes to go fishing, and he indicated that he would bring his dog along with him. The Great Dane is a mellow dog who will be happy to lie next to him while he sits at the lake for hours on end. I suggested that he might want to take him for a trial. He seemed open to the idea but indicated he'd get back to me. If he calls, it's okay to do a conditional adoption."

"Okay, great. And Jigger? Any 'real' men you can think of for him?"

I frowned. Jigger was a sweet dog but a tough placement. He would respond well to a human who was firm but not cruel. If he was placed with someone who wasn't able to maintain the upper hand with him, Jigger would most likely run roughshod over his new owner. On the other hand, if he were placed with a human who ruled with an iron fist, I was afraid the dog could become aggressive.

"I'll need to think about it a bit more. He loves Tank and Gunnar, but I'm not sure they're looking for a permanent roommate. He might do well with Buck Stevenson."

Buck was the new owner of the local lumber mill. He was a man's man, but also a kind and caring soul who tended to assert his dominance with a stern look or firm voice.

"Buck would be perfect." Jeremy smiled. "I'll ask him about it."

I returned to my office and called Zak. What I wanted to do was ask him if he knew that Brooke was in town. What I did ask him was how he was doing with the tape. He reported that he'd had some luck making out portions of the video. He was working on gaining access to the rest, but from what he could see, it looked as if someone had been in the secret passage, taping the entire evening from peepholes drilled into the ceiling of the second floor.

"So the noise Dawn reported hearing from the attic was probably coming from the secret room," I realized.

"It looks like the whole thing was staged," Zak said. "There was definitely someone in the room other than the nine counselors and the as-of-yet unidentified girlfriend. The thing is, the woman who has to be the girlfriend based on the process of elimination looks familiar. From what I've been able to see so far, I'm willing to bet she was working with the cameraman. She isn't drinking or smoking, and she seems to be the one who suggested that the group move to the room where they ended up."

"We need to find that woman."

"Why don't you swing by the house and take a look? You've been in the area longer than I have. Maybe you'll recognize her."

It turned out that I did recognize her. Her name was Tricia. I knew her from a diner where I occasionally have lunch when I'm in Bryton Lake. I called the diner and found out that she got off work at three. I decided to show up as she was getting ready to punch out and ask if she would be willing to go for coffee or something.

"I really appreciate your taking the time to speak with me," I said as I placed our order with the bartender at the saloon down the street from where Tricia worked.

"Hey, if you're willing to buy me all the rum and Coke I want, I'll tell you anything you want to know."

"Great," I responded as the bartender set my glass of water and Tricia's rum and Coke in front of us.

I waited until Tricia had gulped down her first drink and indicated to the bartender that she wanted another before I began.

"I wanted to ask you about your recollection of what happened at the Henderson house thirteen years ago."

Tricia nodded. "Yeah, so you said. What do you want to know?"

"We found a video that was taken the night the counselors died. I recognized you in it from the diner. I know you weren't one of the counselors, so I was wondering why you were at the house that night."

Tricia looked at me. "Guy I met in the park asked me to help him make a video for some film class he was taking. I didn't know what was going to happen."

"Who exactly was it you were helping?" I wondered.

"Like I said, some guy I met in the park. I never did get his name. He was filming people walking by and I thought it was cool, so I stopped to talk to him. He said he was going to make a horror film later that night and asked me if I would help. He offered me a hundred bucks and I wasn't busy, so I agreed."

"Can you remember what he looked like?"

Tricia finished off her second drink. She set her empty glass on the bar and then turned to look at me. "If you want to know every little detail about what happened at the Henderson house, we're going to be in for a pretty long discussion. I don't suppose you want to throw in a pizza and another rum and Coke?"

For the story of what happened the night the counselors died, I'd throw in lobster, but I didn't say as much.

"Okay," I agreed. "How about we move to a booth?"

"Sure."

I placed our order for a small pizza and another drink for Tricia and then joined her in the booth she had chosen at the back of the room. Luckily, at this time of day the bar was nearly deserted, so there were no prying ears to listen in on our conversation.

"So about the guy you were helping . . ." I began as I put down her drink and sat down across from her.

Tricia frowned. "I don't know a lot about him. I met the dude in the park the morning of the party. He asked me to help out, and after I agreed, I followed him up the mountain to that creepy old house. The guy had set up some pranks, and all I had to do was get everyone to gather in one specific room." Tricia looked directly at me. "I had no idea anyone was going to get hurt."

"Yes, so you've said. I'm really not trying to place blame here; I just want to find out what happened."

"Yeah, okay."

"So the film student went up to the secret room when you got there?" I asked.

Tricia looked surprised. "There's a secret room? Cool."

"You didn't know about the room?"

"No," she said. "The guy said he was going upstairs, and that was the last I ever saw of him. When the people from the camp showed up, I suggested we go into the room the dude had indicated

150

I should lead them toward. They all started drinking and things got weird. When the girl got hit in the head with the lamp, I left. I had my own car and the dude had already paid me. I didn't want nothing to do with any prank where people were going to get hurt."

"Did you ever tell anyone about that night?"

"Not that I can remember. Sometimes I get so wasted, I forget pretty much everything that's happened to me. Can I get another drink?"

"Sure, but only if you let me drive you home."

"Yeah, that probably would be best."

When the bartender delivered Tricia's pizza, I asked him to bring another drink. I waited until she had eaten the first slice before continuing.

"So the guy you helped . . . what did you say he looked like?"

"Tall. Skinny. Brown hair, brown eyes, I think. It's been a long time, and to be honest, I've spent the past thirteen years trying to forget the whole thing."

"Would you recognize him now if you saw a photo?" I asked as she dug into her second slice of the cheesy pie just as the bartender brought her fourth—and, as far as I was concerned, last—drink.

Tricia shrugged. "You want a piece of this?" She shoved the half-eaten pizza toward me.

"No thanks. Did you get the feeling that anyone other than you knew they were being filmed?" I asked.

"No, I don't think they knew. I think the pot was laced with something. Everyone was acting really weird."

"Who brought the pot?"

Tricia took a long swig of her drink before answering. "I think the film student brought it. He asked me to pass it around after everyone got settled."

I remembered that Dawn had said that Rachael knew about the pot ahead of time. I wondered if she was in on the prank. Since she was dead, we might never know.

"You said you left after Carol was hit in the head. One of the survivors indicated that the wound didn't seem all that bad."

"It wasn't anything more than a scrape. The chick was passed out from the booze, but she seemed fine when I left. I don't know what happened afterward, but I can assure you that the chick didn't die from her collision with the lamp."

"What did you do when you heard that she'd died?" I had to ask.

"Nothing. I didn't kill her or any of the others and didn't want to get involved. I never told anyone I was even there until today, and I only told you 'cause you said you had a tape. You aren't going to narc to the cops, are you?"

"The cops will see the tape. They'll most likely question you at some point."

"Damn, I need to hit the head. Can you get a box for the rest of that pizza?"

"Yeah, no problem."

Later that evening, after Zak and I had had dinner and settled in front of the fire in the living room with a glass of wine, I decided to bring up the subject that had been plaguing my thoughts throughout the day. Music was playing softly in the background, and part of me hated to ruin the romantic mood with talk of the witch who was in town to steal my Zak, but she'd been on my mind all day and I needed closure.

"Tell me about Brooke Collins."

"I was wondering when you were going to ask about her." Zak sighed in resignation.

"So you know she's in town?"

Zak set his wine down and pulled me into his arms. I rested my head on his shoulder as he caressed my arm. "She called me after you'd left for Bryton Lake. She told me she was in town and that she'd attended the events committee meeting this morning, and she indicated that she'd met you."

"Did she tell you that she was moving to Ashton Falls?"

"She did, but to be honest, I doubt she will. At least not for the long haul. Brooke tends to have a short attention span. My guess is she's here on a whim, and when things don't work out, she'll leave."

I curled my legs up under myself on the sofa and snuggled into Zak's side. "Did she tell you about the auction?"

"She did. In fact, asking me to participate was the reason she called, or at least the reason she gave for calling. She wanted us to get together to talk about the event."

"And what did you say?" I held my breath as I waited for his answer. I'm not sure why his response was so important, but it was.

"I told her that I was in a committed relationship with a woman I loved very much and planned to marry, so therefore I wasn't really single."

I smiled. "Yeah?"

"Yeah." Zak turned and kissed me. I'm not sure how, but somehow I was sure Zak wasn't telling me the whole story. His kiss had a desperation to it.

"There's more."

So I had guessed. I watched the flames flicker as the fire burned down while Zak gathered his thoughts. The rain had returned, giving the room a cozy feel. It seemed such a shame to ruin it with talk about some girl Zak had probably dated once or twice many, many years ago. I was about to suggest we just change the subject when he continued.

"There is more," Zak said again. "Brooke said that I was technically still a bachelor and therefore eligible for the auction. She also reminded me that the money the event would bring in would go a long way toward balancing the town's budget and buying the volunteer force the fire engine it so desperately needs."

Brooke wasn't wrong about the budget.

"I told her there were plenty of single men in town who would be happy to participate, but she pointed out that I was the only single male who was going to draw in the out-of-town crowd with the big bucks. If I didn't participate, we might as well not bother."

I hated to admit it, but Brooke was probably right.

"So where did you leave it?" I asked.

"I told her that my participation was totally up to you."

I was happy Zak hadn't agreed without talking to me about it first, but I hated to be in the position of being the bad guy with the town, which really did need the money.

"You know she only came up with this plan so she could bid on you herself."

"If I agree to do the auction—and I'm not saying that I will—I would make it a stipulation that as event organizer, she would be prohibited from bidding on me or any of the men who volunteer to participate; however, you could always bid on me."

"We both know I can't afford you, and if you give me the money to bid on you, it will look fixed."

"True. Maybe I should just donate the money the volunteer firefighters need," Zak said. "I'm not interested in dating anyone but you."

I laid my head on Zak's shoulder. I was so lucky to have him in my life. I knew he loved me, but I also knew that if I allowed him to, he'd participate for the good of the town.

"If you participate, the other guys in town will also. Chances are that as long as they're there, these women Brooke seems to think she can attract will bid on the others when they realize there's only one of you. If Brooke is correct in her estimation, the town stands to make a *lot* of money. I really don't see how we can pass this up."

Zak turned so he was looking directly at me. "Are you sure?"

I smiled. "I'm sure. As long as Brooke can't win, I think I can deal with you going on a very platonic dinner date if it will help the town. After all, you let me go on a date to help Ellie."

"Yes, I did, didn't I?"

I picked up my wine. There was a little voice in my head screaming at me to move on from the subject of Brooke Collins. I really, really should have listened to that voice. You know what they say about asking questions you don't really want the answers to . . .

"So what exactly is the deal with you and Brooke?" I blurted out in spite of the warning bells and whistles going off in my brain.

Zak hesitated.

"I won't get jealous," I promised.

He still didn't say anything.

"Okay, I probably will get jealous, but I'd rather hear about your relationship from you rather than her. You know she'll tell me if you dated."

"Yes." Zak sighed. "She probably will."

"So you did? Date?"

I was already regretting the fact that I'd brought up the subject. One of these days I'll learn to listen to my instincts.

"Brooke and I met when I was living in Paris, after I sold my company and set off to see the world. We both missed the States, and we got to talking and ended up living together for six months."

"You *lived* together?" I wasn't expecting that.

"Looking back, it was a huge mistake. I didn't love her, at least not like I love you. We did have fun together, and I was feeling displaced after leaving my home and selling the company I'd spent so much of my time building. Brooke brought a sense of the familiar into my life. I needed that familiarity at that point in time."

"What happened?" I wasn't sure I *wanted* to know, but I knew I *needed* to know. "What happened between you?"

I hoped they'd had some huge fight and Zak was going to tell me that they hated each other, but I had the feeling that wasn't it at all. Zak wasn't the type to hate anyone.

"When it came time to move back home, Brooke wanted us to move to New York, and I wanted to move back to Ashton Falls. We couldn't agree on a compromise, so we went our separate ways."

"So you *just* broke up with her before coming home last year?"

"Yes."

"And you didn't think it was important to tell me that you had *just* gotten out of a serious relationship?"

"It wouldn't have made a difference."

"Of course it would have," I spat.

Zak grabbed my shoulders and turned me so that I was looking at him. "Zoe, I love you. I've loved you on some level ever since I met you in the seventh grade. Brooke was a mistake. The moment I saw you after returning home, I knew I could never love anyone other than you. I know I should have told you about Brooke, but I wanted you to love me back so very desperately. I was afraid you would let her get in the way of what we can have together."

"You lied," I accused.

"I didn't lie. You never asked."

I stood up. "I need some time to think about all of this. I'm taking Charlie and going to the boathouse."

# Chapter 13

## Wednesday, October 29

Talk about a truly horrible night. Ellie tried to talk some sense into me when I showed up at the boathouse, but I was furious, so there was no talking to me. I loved Zak and I knew I couldn't let this come between us, but I really didn't know how to handle the raging emotions that were battling inside me. It hurt so much that I wasn't the first woman Zak had cared about enough to live with. How was I going to deal with that knowledge?

"You need to go home and talk to Zak," Ellie encouraged. She'd been great, listening to me rant for most of the night. Neither of us had gotten any sleep, and I knew we both felt like we were running on fumes.

"I know." I sighed. I was so tired.

Ellie handed me a cup of coffee with a touch of milk, just the way I like it when I need something to sooth my stomach while stimulating my mind. "You love him and he loves you. What he did before you got together shouldn't matter."

"I know, but it does."

"Why?" Ellie challenged.

"I don't know; it just does."

"You dated other guys," Ellie reminded me. "You had intimate relationships with other men before you got together with Zak. Those relationships have nothing to do with your feelings for Zak, and I'm sure his relationship with Brooke has nothing to do with his feelings for you."

"Did you know?" I asked.

Ellie looked shocked. "What? How would I know?"

"I don't know, but it occurred to me that you were digging your nails into my leg yesterday to keep me from speaking up at the meeting."

"I knew what Brooke was going to propose," Ellie explained. "I'd gotten to the meeting early and Willa had filled me in. I also knew you'd be jealous, but I knew her idea was good for the town. We need the money Brooke's idea will bring in, and I didn't want you to throw a fit until you had time to think about it. I gathered by what she said that she knew Zak from the past, but I swear to you, I had no idea about the nature of their relationship. I would have told you."

I sighed again. "I know. I'm sorry. I guess I'll go home and talk to Zak."

"I think that would be best."

I hugged Ellie, loaded Charlie into my truck, and headed back to the house Zak and I shared. My heart sank when I noticed that his truck wasn't in the drive. I felt extra bad when I noticed that the Mr. and Mrs. Frankenstein Zak had moved to the yard for the party were lying on the ground in several pieces. I must have plowed them down when I left the night before.

"Zak," I called as I walked through the front door.

No answer.

At least Bella was still there, as was the stray dog we'd begun to refer to as Karloff, after the Boris Karloff movie we'd watched recently. If Zak was going to be gone for long, he would have taken the dogs. Wouldn't he?

I changed into a heavier sweatshirt, then headed back outdoors with all three dogs trailing behind me. I felt bad for putting Zak through what probably had been a very long night. I also felt bad for ruining his display. He'd worked so hard on it. I couldn't undo the stress I'd caused the man I loved, but maybe I could fix the display.

I picked up the pieces that were lying across the drive and repaired what I could. I was going to need help with Frankenstein and his lady, and I knew just who to call. I put on a pot of coffee and considered the mess I'd made of my life while I waited. I'd really thought I had a grip on my often illogical emotions. I'd worked hard to leave behind my insecurities and become a woman worthy of a man like Zak. Apparently, I still had additional work to do.

Life would be so much easier if you could decide how you wanted to feel and your emotions just fell into line. I didn't want to be a jealous, insecure mess who hurts the people she cares most about with childish tantrums and illogical rants, but as hard as I try, I find that the way I want to feel and the way I *do* feel are often not the same.

"You still love me, don't you?" I looked at Charlie as I attempted to rehang the lights in the same artistic manner Zak had so carefully arranged them.

Charlie barked and wagged his tail.

"So what are we going to do with me?"

Charlie cocked his head as if he were trying to understand what I was saying. He put his paw on my leg and licked my cheek when I bent down to pet him.

"Maybe I need to take a lesson from you, my little bundle of unconditional love."

"Thank you for coming," I greeted Joel as he pulled up in front of the house an hour later.

"No problem. I'm happy to help. What exactly is the problem?"

"I'm afraid Frankenstein has been decapitated and the missus isn't doing much better. Can you fix them?"

Joel picked up the pieces and took a closer look. "I don't see why not. I've been working with props since I was a kid. Do you know what happened to the arm?"

The arm? I looked around. I thought I had all the pieces. "I'll check the bushes I ran over on my way out last night."

"A few too many cocktails?" Joel teased.

I blushed.

"Don't worry; I've been there."

I didn't say anything as I carefully began rummaging through the shrubs that were quite a bit worse for wear after my off-road excursion through the middle of them.

"I found the arm," I said, holding it up.

"Is the hand attached?"

It wasn't.

"Bring me the arm and I'll get started on it while you keep looking for the other missing pieces," Joel said.

"You're very good at what you do," I complimented as I watched him begin to reattach the arm. "You could probably get a job doing something with special effects in Hollywood if you wanted."

Joel laughed as he returned to his truck to sort through his tools and supplies. "Thanks, but no thanks. I've done the Hollywood thing. It isn't for me."

"You tried to get a job doing sets?"

"No, I wanted to be a filmmaker. It was my dream during my teens. Once I graduated high school, I began making amateur movies that I sent off to every producer I could get an address for. Eventually, I left this area and headed to Tinsel Town, but things didn't work out, as you can probably guess. I think I can duplicate the missing foot, but we're really going to have to find the original hand if you want it to wave."

Joel turned and looked at me. Suddenly, I knew who was responsible for the deaths all those years ago, and in the split second before he hit me and I blacked out, I realized Joel knew that I knew.

I'm not sure how long I was out, but when I woke up, I was bound and gagged. I recognized my prison as the secret room in the Henderson house. I couldn't hear or see anyone else there, so I hoped Joel had simply left me to die. He didn't know that Zak and I knew about the secret room. My guess was that he planned to leave me there, much the way he had Bart. Of course, he must have noticed that Bart was no longer tucked into his final resting place, so perhaps he planned to come back and finish me off after all.

I tried to work the ropes around my wrists, but they wouldn't budge. I found myself beginning to struggle to breathe as panic set in. I realized that I was hyperventilating, but with the tape over my mouth, I could only breathe through my nose. I knew I needed to get out of there, but the harder I struggled to free my hands and legs, the more difficult it was to catch my breath. I forced myself to close my eyes and stop moving. I needed to relax. Once I returned my breath to a normal pace, I could figure out what to do.

I focused on my breathing as I cleared my head of all but the most positive thoughts. I concentrated on Zak and how much I loved him. I thought about building a life with him and growing old together. I pictured the animals we shared and found myself beginning to panic again as I realized that they had been with me in the yard when Joel knocked me out. I knew that Charlie would have attacked Joel when he hit me. God, I hoped Joel hadn't hurt him.

I tried once again to free my arms. I needed to get home. To Zak; to Charlie; to my life.

The harder I struggled, the shallower my breath became. I forced myself to stop and rest when I began to get dizzy. There was plenty of air in the room. The tape wasn't blocking my nose. I would be fine if I could control my mind and my emotions.

I could hear thunder in the distance. I guess another storm had blown in. The closer the sound of the clattering in the sky, the darker things became. There were no windows in the room, but there had been light coming through the small holes someone had bored. Probably Joel, when he set up the house of horrors for the camp counselors that night. I held my breath as I heard voices below. I prayed it was Zak with Salinger, but I quickly discovered it was Joel, with another man I couldn't see and whose voice I only vaguely recognized.

"If the body is gone, it's only a matter of time until the cops figure this out," the voice I couldn't quite place stated. "We should just leave. Maybe try for another country where we can finally put all this behind us."

"We're in this mess because of you," Joel pointed out.

"Me? What did I do?"

"You didn't control things, so I had to handle them."

"Handle them?" the voice spat. "You call smothering Carol and killing Bart in cold blood *handling things*? I should have gone to the cops a long time ago. If I'd known what you'd done to them, I would have. No one was supposed to get hurt."

"And no one would have gotten hurt if you'd taken care of everything like we agreed. My job was to film the event and your job was to handle the actors."

"They weren't actors. They were just kids who had no idea what was really going on. Your idea to create an actual horror scene had merit, but we didn't stop to consider the very real consequences."

"If you had done your job like we agreed, we would have had our film and no one would have been any the wiser," Joel insisted. "That film could have opened doors for both of us."

"Whatever." I could hear one of the men pacing back and forth. "There's nothing I can do about what happened to the others, but I won't let you kill that girl. We need to let her go and take our punches."

"If you think you'll get off easy by ratting me out, you're dead wrong."

"Put that gun away," the voice who wasn't Joel's demanded. "We're in this together, and we need to accept the consequences of our actions."

"Like hell."

I heard a struggle and then a shot. I would have screamed if my mouth hadn't been taped.

I sat quietly as I waited for the other shoe to drop. Both men seemed to know that I was locked in the room; the question in my mind was, who was the shooter and who was the victim? If Joel had ended up with the gun, chances were that I'd be next. If, however, the owner of the second voice had been the victor, I might be minutes away from being freed.

As the minutes turned to what seemed like hours, I realized that one of the men was most likely dead and the other had probably left. I struggled again to free my wrists. If Joel had killed the other man, he must plan to come back for me. I really needed to get out of there.

I could hear thunder clapping all around. All at once I had an image of a lightning strike hitting the old house and the entire thing becoming engulfed in flames. I found myself beginning to panic again. A rickety old house was nowhere to be trapped in a lightning storm.

I forced myself to calm down and take slow breaths though my nose. Panicking was only going to make things worse. After what seemed like forever, I heard voices once again. My heart began to pound, and I imagined that it was Joel, back to finish the job. Sweat beaded on my forehead as I began to lose control of my breathing. I felt like I was going to vomit, which wouldn't be a good idea considering I had no way of removing the tape from my mouth.

Death by vomit. That was *not* how I wanted to go.

I closed my eyes and mentally forced myself to relax. I heard footsteps on the stairs leading to the attic. I almost passed out from relief when I recognized Zak's voice. When he opened the door to the room and shone his flashlight inside, I began to weep.

"God, Zoe, are you okay?"

Zak ran over to me and wrapped me in his arms.

"Tape," I tried to say through the tape still covering my mouth.

Zak looked at my face and cringed. "I'm sorry. This is going to hurt."

He ripped off the tape and I sucked in the first full breath I'd been able to take since waking up in the secret room.

"What took you so long?" I gasped.

"I didn't know you were here," Zak said as he began to untie my hands. "I went to talk to Brooke this morning and when I came back you weren't home, so I figured you were still at Ellie's."

"But my truck. Charlie?"

"The truck wasn't in the drive. Neither was Charlie."

"Oh God, did Joel hurt Charlie?"

"Charlie is with Scott. Don't worry; Scott swears he'll be fine."

"Get the rest of these ropes off. We have to go."

# Chapter 14

## Thursday, October 30

By the time Zak and I got back from the vet the previous evening, we were both completely exhausted. As I'd predicted, when Joel hit me, Charlie had attacked him, and then Joel had kicked my dog, fracturing a rib. He'd locked Charlie in my truck and then took it down to the dirt road that parallels the lake and left it hidden in some trees. While I quite literally wanted to kill Joel for kicking my dog, I *was* grateful that he hadn't killed him. Neither Bella nor Karloff seemed any worse for wear, and even though the door had been left open, the cats had been safely napping inside throughout the entire ordeal.

When Zak got home, he'd noticed that Bella and Karloff were sitting on the front porch. The front door was cracked open, so he'd figured he hadn't closed it all the way when he left and the dogs had simply gotten out. Zak didn't realize I wasn't still at Ellie's until he decided to go over there to talk to me and she informed him that I'd gone home early that morning.

When he got home from Ellie's, he looked around. Really looked around. He noticed that someone had cleaned things up and moved parts of Mr. and Mrs. Frankenstein. After a bit of thought, he'd put two and two together. He pulled up the calls that had been made on our landline that day, and when he'd realized that I'd called Joel, he'd logged onto his computer and tracked the signal put off by my truck's communication system. Once he found Charlie and the otherwise empty truck, he'd called Scott and Salinger and then come looking for me in the one place he figured Joel would take me.

"I've never been so scared in all my life," Zak said as we lay in each other's arms after sleeping for a good twelve hours.

"I know. Me neither. I'm so sorry about everything. If I hadn't let my jealousy get the better of me, none of this would have happened."

Zak kissed the top of my head where it rested on his bare chest. "No, it's my fault. I should have told you about Brooke. At first we didn't really have a relationship, so it didn't seem relevant. And then, when our flirtation moved toward something more, I was afraid you would be upset. I thought about telling you, but I was afraid it would destroy what we were just building. But now that I've had a chance to really think about it, I know in my heart we would have worked things out. I promise I'll never keep anything from you again."

I reached up and kissed Zak on the lips. "I was really scared when I got home and you were gone," I admitted.

Zak caressed my hair, which had grown long enough to create a curtain around us. I'd thought about getting it cut, but when you have a thick curly mess that has to be clipped back most of the time anyway, it doesn't seem worth the effort.

"I guess I should have called you or texted or left a note or something," Zak said. "I wasn't thinking clearly. I just knew I had to do what I could to fix things, so I went to see Brooke to ask her to leave Ashton Falls. I needed to make sure she understood that there was absolutely no future for us. I'm in love with you. I want to marry you. I have no interest in dating anyone other than you. Ever."

I smiled. "Did she leave?"

"I'm not sure. She made a case for this being a free country, so she could live wherever she wanted and there was nothing I could do about it. If you want my opinion, I think she was just being difficult because she was hurt that I no longer wanted her in my life. If she hasn't left yet, I'm sure she will once she realizes that I am most definitely not available."

"But the auction? We really do need the money."

"We'll get it another way."

I leaned down to kiss Zak. I really wished we could spend the day making up, but I knew we couldn't. It was already late in the morning, and I had promises I needed to keep.

"As much as I hate to say this, we really need to get going." I sighed. "I promised Salinger I'd be in to make a statement before noon, and I want to go get Charlie."

Zak had been right. Charlie would be fine, but Scott had wanted to keep him overnight to monitor his vitals, just in case there was no internal bleeding or a head wound not immediately apparent.

Zak kissed me one more time. "Okay, let's go get Charlie. It's just not the same around here without him."

"I suppose we should check on Drake. He's probably responsible for the fact that I was still alive when you found me."

"I'll call the hospital to see if he's allowed visitors," Zak suggested. "There's no use going over there if he isn't."

"That's true. I suppose Salinger has a guard on him. I'm sure they'll move him to a secure facility as soon as he's stable. I know he kept a huge secret all these years, but I really hope the DA goes easy on him. He could have just left me to die at Joel's hands."

"We'll make sure Salinger knows what he did for you."

It turned out that Drake Bollinger's had been the other voice I'd heard at the Henderson house. Filming the video thirteen years ago had been the joint effort of Joel and Drake, both film enthusiasts. Joel had convinced Drake that if they wanted to make an authentic horror movie, they needed the actors to be genuinely scared, so they'd enticed the counselors to come to the house for a party. None of the counselors except Drake knew that the spooky happenings had been choreographed.

"I'll go down to take care of the animals while you grab a shower," Zak added.

"We could shower together," I flirted.

"If we do, I guarantee you won't make your meeting with Salinger."

"Oh, very well. I'll be down in less than twenty minutes. It would be wonderful if you started the coffee while you're downstairs."

"Already on it."

That evening, I sat with Zak and Charlie while Levi and Ellie sat on the adjoining sofa. Bella and Shep lay at Ellie's feet, Karloff was snuggled on the sofa next to Levi, Marlow was curled in Zak's lap, and Spade hung out with Ellie. It was so nice to have the whole family together. I know that if I'd died in that secret room, my ghostly self would really miss the *us* we'd become.

"So Joel was the mastermind behind this whole thing," Levi stated. "Who would have thought?"

"I was pretty surprised myself when all the pieces fell into place. I've known him a long time and he really never seemed like the type to be so evil. In fact, prior to all of this happening, I would be the first to say he was a really nice guy."

"I guess sometimes circumstances can compel a nice guy to act in a not so nice manner," Ellie suggested. "If things had gone differently and no one had died that night thirteen years ago, Joel might never have ventured over to the dark side."

"I don't know," Levi countered. "I think the dark side has to be lurking around in the first place in order to rear its ugly head. Drake took a bullet rather than let Joel hurt Zoe. If circumstance was the only variable, he could just as easily have let her die in order to keep his secret."

"True," Ellie acknowledged.

"I really believe that initially neither man meant for anyone to get hurt, but after Rachael fell down the stairs and broke her neck and George was killed by Griff's car, Joel freaked out and things spun out of control," I added.

"So Joel killed the missing counselor?" Levi clarified.

"Drake told Salinger that Joel confessed to killing Bart in order to keep him quiet. I guess after everyone ran outside, Bart realized Carol had been left behind. When he went back inside the house to get her, Joel was standing over her body. It seems Carol, who was still alive, was just starting to come out of it when everyone started panicking. Once Bart realized that there had been someone else on the premises the whole time, he figured out what had happened. He told Joel that his little prank had caused the death of two people, and he was going to the police with the truth. Joel killed him. Carol had heard everything, so Joel smothered her in order to keep her quiet."

"God, it really was all so tragic." Levi sighed. "Not only did perfectly normal people commit truly heinous acts, but there were quite a few people who lived quietly with the memory for all these years. It seems almost incomprehensible."

"What's really strange is that a thirteen-year-old murder mystery was solved by digging into a modern-day accident," Ellie commented. "So Drake is going to be okay?"

"It looks like he will," I confirmed.

Zak got up to toss another log on the fire. I felt myself begin to drift off as fatigue set in. Charlie was curled up next to me, and as I felt his little heart beating with the palm on my hand, I knew I would never take the people and animals I loved for granted again.

"So no one other than Joel knew that he killed Bart and hid his body in the secret room," Levi was saying.

"As far as I can tell," I answered. "After Davenport came back to town and started snooping around, Drake called Joel and insisted that they come clean about what had happened that night. Of course, he still believed Bart simply had taken off and Carol had died from a blow to the head. He'd never said anything in all those years, but he was afraid Davenport was going to figure things out. Joel said they couldn't go to the authorities, but Drake argued that everything that went down thirteen years ago was just a terrible accident, and they should accept responsibility for keeping the secret all these years. It was then that Joel filled Drake in on exactly what had occurred with both Bart and Carol. Drake still wanted to go to the sheriff's office, but Joel threatened him, so he came to Ashton Falls to try to talk Davenport into leaving the area. By the time he got here, it was too late. Joel had used the props he already had on site for the haunted barn to scare Davenport into falling down the stairs and then hoped that everyone would believe what they did: that the whole thing was simply an unfortunate accident."

"Then Drake confronted Joel after he kidnapped you and Joel shot him," Ellie pieced together. "The question is, how did Drake know that Joel had kidnapped you?"

"Good question. I guess I'll have to ask him."

"I'm glad he did. Save your life, that is," Ellie said.

"Can I get anyone more wine?" Zak asked.

"No, but I'll take some coffee and some of that cake I brought," Ellie answered.

"I'll take a beer, if you have one," Levi added.

"I'm fine." I smiled

When Zak got up to get the beverages, Charlie thumped his tail, and I coaxed him into staying with me rather than following him and Bella into the kitchen. Scott had assured me that Charlie would be fine, but he wanted me to keep him quiet for a few days.

"So what now?" Levi asked as Karloff snored in his lap.

"Salinger has put out an APB on Joel, and I'm sure Drake is looking at some sort of consequence for his role in the whole thing once he gets out of the hospital. Salinger knows Drake tried to help me and ended up shot for his efforts, so I have the feeling they'll work out some sort of deal. Right now, I just want to relax and enjoy what remains of the Halloween season."

"What are you going to do about the party?" Ellie wondered.

"I'm not sure. I really want to spend the evening with my friends and family, but Scott recommended that I keep Charlie quiet for a few days, so I'm not sure how that's going to work with a house full of people."

"I suppose you could postpone the party for a few days," Ellie said. "Zak worked so hard on the decorations, it would be a shame to waste all that effort completely."

"We could do a Spook-vember party next weekend," Levi suggested.

The idea had merit. "I'll ask Zak what he thinks."

"Thinks about what?" Zak asked, coming back with the refreshments.

"Postponing the party until next weekend and renaming it the first annual Spook-vember Spectacular."

"I'm not sure I'd want to do it in November every year, but postponing it this year sounds fine with me. It might be better than trying to do it tomorrow as planned. We really should keep Charlie quiet like Scott recommended. Hopefully, the little guy will be back to his old self by next weekend."

"I'll call everyone tomorrow morning," Ellie proposed. "I have the guest list we made up last month, unless you've added anyone to it since then."

"I'll take a look at the list, but it should be pretty accurate," I said.

"School is out for the holiday, so I can help," Levi offered.

"That would be nice." Ellie smiled.

"So about Karloff . . ." I looked directly at Levi. "He seems to really like you."

Levi grinned. "I was wondering how long it was going to take you to thrust the little guy off on me."

"Levi doesn't do babies of any kind," Ellie reminded me.

"Now, hold on. I never said I didn't like babies. I might not be quite ready for a real baby, but I have to admit this little guy is working his way into my heart. He's really pretty cute, plus I bet he'd be the perfect chick magnet."

"Why do you need a chick magnet when you have Darla?" Ellie asked.

"Darla and I have decided not to see each other anymore. We're still friends, but we both wanted to see other people, so it was a mutual agreement."

"So you'd consider taking him?" I asked.

"Maybe," Levi hedged. "Can I take him for a few days and see how it works out?"

"Absolutely."

# Chapter 15

## Halloween

"I'm sorry we had to postpone the party, but this is nice." I was snuggled on the sofa with Zak. Charlie was lying next to me, sound asleep and dreaming about adventures in doggie land. Bella was lying at our feet, and both Marlow and Spade had decided to curl up on the back of the sofa. The room was dark except for the light from the fire and the Halloween decorations.

"This apple éclair cake Ellie dropped off is to die for," I commented as I slowly chewed the last bite.

"It would be good with other kinds of filling as well," Zak commented.

"Is there enough left to offer to our little band of trick-or-treaters when they come by?" I asked.

"Yeah, Ellie brought two cakes. I was going to put one in the freezer, but I'll save it to serve when your parents get here. And speaking of your parents . . ." Zak began, "we need to talk about something before they get here."

*Uh-oh.* That didn't sound good at all.

"Is something wrong?" I asked.

"No, nothing's wrong. It's just that . . ." Zak paused.

It was a *long* pause. Long pauses were never good news. I felt my stomach muscles tighten.

"Just tell me."

"Your dad came by today while you were at the vet with Charlie for his follow-up. I guess the guys at the firehouse were really disappointed to hear that the bachelor auction was off. The single guys were actually looking forward to the auction and . . . well, you know they really need a new truck."

I felt my heart sink, but I didn't say anything. I was determined to kill off Jealous Zoe once and for all. Not only did she threaten my relationship with the man I love more than life itself, but she almost got me killed. Again.

"We *do* need a new truck," I choked out.

"Your dad asked me if I would be willing to reconsider participating in the auction if we made a few changes."

"Changes?"

Zak took a deep breath. I could see he was nervous about having this discussion. "We'd find a new organizer, for one. I insisted that the only way I would even consider the plan was if we did it without Brooke."

I smiled. "I appreciate that, but she did have a point. We're only going to make the kind of money we need for a new fire engine if we can bring in the high-society clientele she promised. The women in this town couldn't afford to spend thousands of dollars on a date even if they wanted to. Without the women Brooke can bring in, the whole thing will be a bust."

"That's true, but I think your dad has someone in mind to take Brooke's place. Someone who makes Brooke look like a guppy in a shark pond when it comes to high-society connections."

I know I must have looked confused because Zak continued without waiting for me to catch up.

"Your mom."

"My mom. Of course. I keep forgetting who she is. During the past few months, I've gotten so used to her just being my mom that I forget she used to be Madison Montgomery, socialite extraordinaire. So what did you tell Dad?"

"I told him that I'd talk to you about it. They still want me to be the headliner, so I'll still need to go on a date. A very platonic date," Zak assured me.

Zak waited while I considered the situation. The town needed the money the event would bring in, and it made sense to utilize the fourth most eligible bachelor in the country when we had him at our fingertips. I trusted Zak and wasn't really all that concerned about another woman bidding on him. And if my mom ran things, you could bet she'd put together a classy affair and would invite women who had altruism rather than boyfriend stealing on their minds.

"Okay," I agreed as the doorbell rang, announcing my family's arrival.

"You're sure?"

"I'm sure. Let's go see how adorable Harper looks in her Halloween costume. Get the camera."

I jogged over to the door and opened it. The porch was filled with people I loved dressed to celebrate my favorite holiday. The world suddenly felt like a wonderful place.

"Oh my gosh, aren't you all so adorable," I cooed as Harper, Morgan, and Ava, all dressed in Halloween costumes, greeted me. Of course, they were only six months old, so they were all held by their respective mothers, and none seemed to care about the candy I slipped into the plastic pumpkins their parents were holding. I took Harper into my arms and cuddled her to my chest.

"Take our picture," I instructed Zak. I wanted to remember every detail of Harper's first Halloween. In spite of the impending bachelor auction, I couldn't remember the last time I'd been this happy.

"Come in, all of you," I invited. "I need tons of photos to remember this special event. Where are Jessica and Rosalie?"

"Rosalie has a cold, so Morgan and I are going to bring Halloween to them after we finish here," Jeremy explained. "I knew you'd kill me if I didn't bring Morgan by first."

"You were right, I would have. Don't leave without taking a goodie bag for Rosalie. I made up something special."

Unlike the babies, Rosalie, at five, would love the treats and gifts I'd prepared.

"There's wine and some of the delicious cake Ellie made on the table. Help yourselves while I get my photos."

Luckily, all three babies were in good moods and were happy to pose while Zak and I took photos and their parents drank Zak's expensive wine.

"Did Zak talk to you?" Dad asked after I had taken enough photos to fill twenty albums.

"He did. Why didn't you?"

Dad blushed.

"You were afraid I'd flip out and bite your head off," I guessed.

"You do have a bit of a temper."

"I know." I kissed him on the cheek. "I love the idea of Mom organizing a bachelor auction. I bet she has tons of good ideas."

"You know your mom; once I suggested it, she went into full party-planner mode. She'd like to have it before Thanksgiving, so that won't give us much time. If you're okay with the idea, I'll give her the go-ahead to start calling the people she wants to handle the flowers, catering, and decorating. She's already made up a list of women to invite. My guess is that most of the women will go out of their way to attend a Madison Montgomery party. She even has several magazines that have expressed interest in sending photographers if we manage to pull the whole thing together."

"You do realize that with Mom in charge, it's going to cost almost as much to produce this shindig as we're likely to make. Zak and Mom could easily go in together to buy a new engine and save everyone the work."

"The guys need to feel like they contributed."

Dad was right. The volunteer firefighters, as well as the other men in the community, would get the satisfaction of earning the equipment they needed rather than having it handed to them.

"Okay," I said, "I'm in."

Dad hugged me. "I knew you would do the right thing."

"Don't I always?"

"Yes." Dad smiled. "In the end, you always do."

After everyone left and it was just Zak and the animals and me, I browsed through the photos I'd taken. Harper was so very cute in her itty-bitty witch outfit, as were the other babies in their little costumes. In my heart, I know that someday I want to have a baby of my own. Zak's baby.

I could feel Zak's arm against my own as we thumbed through the photos he'd brought up on his new tablet. There was no doubt in my mind that he was the only man I would ever want to spend my life with. I don't know why I'm having such a hard time making a commitment. Time wouldn't change what I already knew in my heart to be true.

Zak pointed to the funny face Morgan had made when we tried to get her to hold a tiny pumpkin we'd carved. My baby sister Harper had grinned like the cat who got the cream when we handed it to her, but Morgan was just a tad more suspicious of the strange item. Harper seemed to glow in every photo we managed to snap. There was no doubt about it; Harper was going to be Halloween crazy like her big sister.

I looked at Zak as he made a comment about each photo I'd taken. I realized that sometimes, when you find the person who you know to be the other half of your heart, you just have to take a blind leap of faith that things will work out the way they're intended.

Maybe it was the romance, the firelight, the fun family evening, the upcoming bachelor auction, or the fact that I had almost died (again), but I found myself saying yes.

"Yes?" Zak asked without looking up from the tablet, where he was manipulating the photos.

"Yes, I'll marry you."

I held my breath, heart pounding, as I waited for a reply.

Zak looked up. "Really?"

"Uh, yeah, really."

Zak smiled. "And you're sure about this?"

"I'm sure." I felt myself begin to hyperventilate.

"Breathe," Zak instructed as he held my shoulders and looked me directly in the eye. "I love you, and you know I want to marry you, but I want you to know that I'll wait if you need more time."

I took a deep breath. "I don't need more time. I'm ready. I want to do this."

Zak pulled me into his arms and showed me just how much he loved me.

A long while later, we were snuggled up in bed watching the fire and listening to the rain. All the animals were sleeping in various locations around the room. I knew this was one of the most perfect moments that would ever happen in my life. I wanted to cherish everything about this special night. I wanted to remember every detail.

"Were you thinking of a long engagement?" Zak asked as he mindlessly traced a figure eight on my shoulder. The fire had burned down, leaving an orange glow that created a feeling of warmth in the room.

I thought about Zak's question as I inhaled the scent from the pumpkin candle I'd lit and listened to *All Of Me* by John Legend as it played on the home entertainment system. All of me *did* love all of him, but was I really ready for this? I snuggled my cheek against Zak's bare chest as I traced our initials with my index finger. I could hear his heart beating, which filled me with a sense of peace and contentment. Of course I was ready for this. I loved Zak and wanted to be his wife.

"I wasn't necessarily thinking of a long engagement," I eventually answered.

"So short?"

"Well, not *too* short. I mean, I'd like a while to get used to the idea. And there are plans to make," I pointed out.

"So are we talking months?" Zak fished.

"Perhaps." I stopped tracing and looked up at him. "Although I suppose there are advantages to taking things slow."

"How slow?" Zak tucked a lock of my hair, which had been covering my eyes, behind my ear.

"I don't know. Slow." I paused to think about it. Maybe I did need a little more time. "The more I think about it, the more I think a long engagement is the way to go."

"So glacial?"

"Exactly." I grinned. "You know me so well."

"Yes, I do." Zak leaned down and kissed me eagerly on the lips.

"And you're okay with taking things slow?" I asked when we came up for air.

"I'm okay with whatever you want."

"Good. Then maybe we should wait to set an actual date. There really isn't any reason to rush into things." I snuggled into Zak's side.

"So are we telling people?" Zak asked as he arranged his arms around me.

"Of course, silly. What's the point of being engaged if you don't tell anyone?"

"Does that mean a formal announcement?" Zak asked hesitantly.

"Well, I wasn't thinking we'd put an announcement in the paper or anything."

"So friends?" Zak gently stroked my hair.

"Of course. Eventually," I added as my heart started to pound. All of a sudden, everything was becoming real, and I was pretty sure I was going to have a panic attack. What in the heck was wrong with me?

"I was thinking," Zak lifted himself onto one arm and looked into my eyes, "that maybe we should wait until we get a ring to tell anyone. I mean, why make an announcement it you don't have a ring to show off?"

I took a deep breath. My heart rate slowed. "A ring? Of course we can't tell anyone until we get a ring." I felt myself relax. "And with the holidays . . ."

"It could be a while until we have a chance to shop," Zak added.

"But *we* know. You and I. We know, and when we're ready, we'll tell everyone."

"When *you're* ready, we'll tell everyone." Zak leaned down to kiss me. "Until then, I think we should focus on other things newly engaged couples focus on."

"I like the way you think."

# Recipes for Haunted Hamlet

Apple Pie Biscuits
Cheesy White Chicken Enchiladas
Chicken Ruben Casserole
Loaded Mashed Potato French Bread
Cheesy Ham and Potato Soup
Pumpkin Cookies

# Apple Pie Biscuits

**Directions:**

Preheat oven to 375 degrees.

Spray a 6 x 9 baking dish on all sides with nonstick spray.

Open 1 can large buttermilk biscuits (I use Pillsbury Grands!)

Melt 1 stick (½ cup) butter (I melt it in a bowl in the microwave)

Combine in a bowl:

½ cup white sugar
½ cup brown sugar
1 tsp. nutmeg
1 tbs. cinnamon

Prepare biscuits:

Dip each biscuit into butter coating on both sides, then dip each biscuit into sugar mixture, coating on both sides. Place into baking dish.

The topping:

Top with one can of apple pie filling.

Combine remaining butter with remaining sugar mixture. Add ½ cup oatmeal and 1 cup chopped pecans. Pour over top of biscuits.

Bake at 375 degrees for 35 minutes.

Drizzle over top when baked:

Combine:

1 cup powdered sugar
¼ cup heavy cream

Serve hot.

# Cheesy White Chicken Enchiladas

Preheat oven to 350 degrees.

Spray 9 x 13 baking dish with nonstick spray.

Mix in a bowl:

3 large chicken breasts, cooked and cubed
1 cup sour cream
8 oz. diced green chiles (Ortega)

Fill 8 medium flour tortillas with chicken filling.

Sauce:

In a medium saucepan combine:

1 cube butter, melt over medium heat
4 oz. cream cheese, add to melted butter and stir until smooth
1 cup heavy whipping cream, stir until blended
1½ cups grated parmesan, stir in slowly to avoid lumps

Pour over tortillas and top with 16 oz. Monterey Jack cheese, grated.

Bake uncovered at 350 degrees for 20–25 minutes.

Broil for a few minutes to brown.

# Chicken Ruben Casserole

Grease 9 x 13 casserole dish. Place in dish 6–8 boneless and skinless chicken breasts (depending on size).

Cover chicken with 16 oz. sauerkraut; squeeze out excess fluid.

Place one slice Swiss cheese over each chicken breast.

Cover with Thousand Island dressing (about 1½ cups).

Bake at 350 degrees for 60 minutes.

# Loaded Mashed Potato French Bread

16 oz. loaf of French bread
1 stick butter, melted
3 lbs. russet potatoes
¼ cup sour cream
1 cup shredded cheddar cheese
6 strips cooked bacon, crumbled
1 bunch green onions, chopped

Preheat the oven broiler.

Hollow out the bread loaf to create a canoelike shape. Brush the inside of the bread loaf with butter and brown under the broiler until barely brown.

Boil and mash the potatoes.

Stir in the rest of the melted butter, sour cream, cheese, bacon, and green onions.

Pour the mashed potatoes into the bread loaf.

Turn the oven to 350 degrees and bake until the bread is golden brown and forms a nice crust.

Serve with grilled chicken or steak.

**Tips:**

The mashed potatoes can be made the day before and heated before pouring into the bread loaf.

You can make individual portions by using hollowed-out Kaiser rolls.

Real packaged bacon bites can be used in place of bacon, or you can use leftover bacon from breakfast.

# Cheesy Ham and Potato Soup

Combine in stockpot:

4 large potatoes (8–9 cups), washed, peeled, and cubed
2–3 large carrots, washed and sliced
1 small onion, finely chopped
4 cups cooked ham, cubed
8 cups chicken broth

Bring to boil and cook until potatoes are tender.

In separate pan:

Melt one cube of butter (½ cup).

Add 3 cups of heavy cream.

Add 3 cups of grated cheddar cheese.

Slowly add 1 cup of Parmesan cheese.

Salt and pepper to taste

When potatoes are cooked through, break them up with a fork or masher. Slowly add cream mixture, stirring constantly.

I use additional Parmesan to thicken or additional milk to thin, if needed.

This soup is really best served the next day, but it's yummy the day of as well.

# Pumpkin Cookies

Cream together:

1 cube margarine, softened
½ cup sugar

Add and mix thoroughly:

½ cup dark corn syrup
1 cup canned pumpkin
1 egg beaten
1 tsp. vanilla

Add to pumpkin mixture and mix thoroughly:

2 cups flour
1 tsp. baking soda
½ tsp. salt
1 tsp. vanilla

Stir in:

I cup chopped walnuts

Drop onto greased cookie sheet. Flatten with fork.

Bake at 375 degrees for about 15 minutes (or until browned).

Cool and frost.

**Frosting:**

¾ cup butter, softened
6 oz. cream cheese, softened
1 tbs. vanilla
3 cups powdered sugar

# Books by Kathi Daley

## Paradise Lake Series:

Pumpkins in Paradise
Snowmen in Paradise
Bikinis in Paradise
Christmas in Paradise – *September 2014*

## Zoe Donovan Mysteries:

Halloween Hijinks
The Trouble With Turkeys
Christmas Crazy
Cupid's Curse
Big Bunny Bump-off
Beach Blanket Barbie
Maui Madness
Derby Divas
Haunted Hamlet
Turkeys, Tuxes, and Tabbies – *October 2014*
Christmas Cozy – *November 2014*

## Road to Christmas Romance:

Road to Christmas Past

Kathi Daley lives with her husband, kids, grandkids, and Bernese mountain dogs in beautiful Lake Tahoe. When she isn't writing, she likes to read (preferably at the beach or by the fire), cook (preferably something with chocolate or cheese), and garden (planting and planning, not weeding). She also enjoys spending time on the water when she's not hiking, biking, or snowshoeing the miles of desolate trails surrounding her home.

Kathi uses the mountain setting in which she lives, along with the animals (wild and domestic) that share her home, as inspiration for her cozy mysteries.

Stay up to date with her newsletter, *The Daley Weekly*. There's a link to sign up on both her Facebook page and her website, or you can access the sign-in sheet at: http://eepurl.com/NRPDf

Visit Kathi:

Facebook at Kathi Daley Books, www.facebook.com/kathidaleybooks

Twitter at Kathi Daley@kathidaley

Webpage www.kathidaley.com

E-mail kathidaley@kathidaley.com

SEP 1 2 2014

SOUTH LAKE TAHOE

Made in the USA
San Bernardino, CA
03 August 2014